# THE WHITE SQUAW.

"HALF CARRYING, HALF SUPPORTING, HE CONDUCTED HIM TO THE CANOE."

No. 1.

# THE WHITE SQUAW:

## AN INDIAN TALE.

### CHAPTER I.

#### A DEADLY INTRODUCTION.

THE last golden rays of the setting sun sparkled across the translucent waters of Tampa Bay. This fading light fell upon shores fringed with groves of oak and magnolia, whose evergreen leaves became gradually darkened by the purple twilight.

A profound silence, broken by the occasional notes of a tree-frog, or the flapping of the nighthawk's wings, was but the prelude to that wonderful concert of animated nature heard only in the tropical forest.

A few moments, and the golden lines of trembling light had disappeared, while darkness almost palpable overshadowed the scene.

Then broke forth in full chorus the nocturnal voices of the forest.

The mocking bird, the whip-poor-will, the bittern, the bell frog, grasshoppers, wolves, and alligators, all joined in the harmony incident to the hour of night, causing a din startling to the ear of a stranger.

Now and then would occur an interval of silence, which rendered the renewal of the voices all the more observable.

During one of these pauses a cry might have been heard differing from all the other sounds.

It was the voice of a human being, and there was one who heard it.

Making his way through the woods was a young man, dressed in half-hunter costume, and carrying a rifle in his hand.

The cry had caused him to stop suddenly in his tracks.

After glancing cautiously around, as if endeavouring to pierce the thick darkness, he again advanced, again came to a stop, and remained listening.

Once more came that cry, in which accents of anger were strangely commingled with tones appealing for help.

This time the sound indicated the direction, and the listener's resolution was at once taken.

Thrusting aside the undergrowth, and trampling under foot the tall grass, he struck into a narrow path running parallel to the shore, and which led in the direction whence the cry appeared to have come.

Though it was now quite dark, he seemed easily to avoid impediments, which even in broad daylight would have been difficult to pass.

The darkness appeared no barrier to his speed, and neither the overhanging branches, nor the wild bine roots stayed his progress.

About a hundred paces further on, the path widened into a list that led to an opening sloping gradually down to the beach.

On reaching its edge, he paused once more to listen for a renewal of the sound.

Nothing save the familiar noises of the night greeted his ear.

After a short pause, he kept on for the water's edge, with head well forward, and eyes strained to penetrate the gloom.

At that moment the moon shot out from behind a heavy bank of clouds, and, with a brilliant beam, disclosed to his eager gaze a tableau of terrible interest.

Down by the water's edge lay the body of an Indian youth, motionless, and to all appearance dead; while stooping over it was another youth, also an Indian.

He appeared to be examining the body.

For some seconds there was no change in his attitude.

Then all at once he raised himself erect, and with a tomahawk that flashed in the moonlight above his head, appeared in the act of dealing a blow.

The hatchet descended; but not upon the body that lay prostrate.

A sharp report ringing on the air for an instant silenced all other sounds.

The would-be assassin sprang up almost simultaneously, and two corpses instead of one lay along the earth.

So thought he who had fired the shot, and who was the young man already described.

He stayed not to speculate, but rushed forward to the spot where the two Indians lay.

He had recognised them both.

The one upon the ground was Nelatu, the son of Oluski, a distinguished Seminole chief.

The other was Red Wolf, a well-grown youth belonging to the same tribe.

Only glancing at the would-be assassin to see that he was dead, he bent over the body of Nelatu, placed his hand upon the region of his heart, at the same time anxiously scanning his features.

Suddenly he uttered an exclamation of surprise.

Beneath his fingers a weak pulsation gave signs of life.

Nelatu might yet be saved.

Pulling off his hat, he ran down to the beach, filled it with water, and, returning, sprinkled the forehead of the young Indian.

Then taking a flask containing brandy from his pouch, he poured a portion of its contents down the throat of the unconscious youth.

These kindly offices he repeated several times, and was finally rewarded for his pains.

The blood slowly mantled Nelatu's cheek; a shiver ran through his frame; and with a deep sigh, he gazed dreamily upon his preserver, at the same time faintly murmuring "Warren."

"Yes, Warren! Speak, Nelatu! What is the meaning of this?"

The Indian had only the strength to mutter the words "Red Wolf," at the same time raising his hand to his side with apparent difficulty.

The gesture made his meaning clear.

Warren's gaze rested upon a deep wound from which the blood was still welling.

By the tremulous movement of his lips, Warren saw that he was endeavouring to speak again.

But no sound came from them.

His eyes gradually became closed.

He had once more fainted.

Warren instantly flung off his coat, tore one of the sleeves from his shirt, and commenced staunching the blood.

After a time it ceased to flow, and then tearing off the second sleeve, with his braces knotted together, he bound up the wound.

The wounded youth slowly recovered consciousness, and looking gratefully up into his face, pressed the hand of his deliverer.

"Nelatu owes Warren life. He will some day show his gratitude."

"Don't think of that now. Tell me what has happened. I heard your cry, and hastened to your assistance."

"Not Nelatu's cry," responded the Indian, with a faint blush of pride suffusing his face. "Nelatu is the son of a chief. He knows how to die without showing himself a woman. It was Red Wolf who cried out."

"Red Wolf!"

"Yes; Red Wolf is a coward—a squaw; 'twas he who cried out."

"He will never cry out again. Look there!" said Warren, pointing to the lifeless corpse that lay near.

Nelatu had not yet seen it.

Unconscious of what had transpired, he believed that Red Wolf, supposing him dead, had gone away from the spot.

Warren explained.

Still more gratefully did the Indian youth gaze upon the face of his preserver.

"You had an encounter with Red Wolf? I can see that of course; it was he who gave you this wound?"

"Yes, but I had first defeated him. I had him on the ground in my power. I could have taken his life; it was then, that, like a coward, he called for help."

"And after?"

"I pitied him and let him rise. I expected him to leave me, and go back to the village. He feared that I might speak of his defeat to our tribe, and he determined that my tongue should be for ever silent. I was not thinking of it when he thrust me from behind. You know the rest."

"And why the quarrel?"

"He spoke wicked words of my sister, Sansuta."

"Sansuta!" exclaimed Warren, a

strange smile overshadowing his features.

"Yes; and of you."

"The dog! then he doubly deserved death. And from *me!*" he added, in a tone not loud enough for Nelatu to hear, "what a lucky chance."

As he said this, he spurned the body with his foot.

Then turning to the Indian, he asked—

"Do you think you could walk a little, Nelatu?"

The brandy had by this time produced an effect.

Its potent spirit supplied the loss of blood, and Nelatu felt his strength returning to him.

"I will try," said the wounded youth. "Nelatu's hour has not yet come. He must not die till he has paid his debt to Warren."

"Then lean on me. My canoe is close by. Once in it, you can rest at your ease."

Nelatu nodded consent.

Warren assisted him to rise, and, half carrying, half supporting, conducted him to the canoe.

Carefully helping him aboard, he shoved the craft from the shore, and turned its prow in the direction of the white settlement.

The moon, that had become again obscured, once more burst through the black clouds, lighting up the fronds of the feathery palms that flung their graceful shadows far over the pellucid waves.

The concert of the nocturnal forest, for a time stayed by the report of the rifle, burst out anew as the boat glided silently out of sight.

---

## CHAPTER II.

### THE SETTLEMENT.

THE site of the settlement to which the canoe was being directed merits description.

It was upon the northernmost shore of Tampa Bay.

The soil that had been cleared was rich in crops of cotton, indigo, sugar, and the ordinary staples of food.

Through the cultivated lands, mapped out like a painter's palette, ran a crystal stream, from which the rice fields were watered by intersecting rivulets, looking like silver threads in a tissue.

Orange groves margined its course, running sinuously through the settlement.

In places it was lost to sight, only to reappear with some new feature of beauty.

Here and there it exhibited cascades and slight waterfalls that danced in the sunlight, sending up showers of prismatic spray.

There were islets upon which grew

reeds, sedges and canes, surmounted by groups of caricas, and laurel-magnolias, the exogenous trees overtopped by the tall, feathery palm.

In its water wild fowl disported themselves, scattering showers of luminous spray as they flapped their wings in delight.

Birds of rare plumage darted hither and thither along its banks, enlivening the groves with their jocund notes.

Far beyond, the swamp forest formed a dark, dreary background, which, by contrast, enhanced the cheerfulness of the scene.

Looking seaward, the prospect was no less resplendent of beauty.

The water, dashing and fretting against the rocky quays, glanced back in mist and foam.

Snow-white gulls hurried along the horizon, their wings cutting sharply against an azure sky, while along the silvery beach, tall, blue herons, brown cranes, and scarlet flamingoes, stood in rows, their forms reflected in the pellucid element.

Such were the surroundings of the settlement on Tampa Bay.

The village itself nestled beneath the hills already mentioned, and comprised a church, some half-dozen stores, with a number of substantial dwellings, whilst a rude wharf, and several schooners, moored near by, gave tokens of intercourse with other places.

It was a morning in May, in Florida, as elsewhere, the sweetest month of the year.

Borne upon the balmy atmosphere was the hum of bees and the melody of birds, mingled with the voices of young girls and men engaged in the labour of their farms and fields.

The lowing of cattle could be heard in the distant grazing grounds, while the tillers of the soil were seen at work upon their respective plantations.

There was one who looked upon this cheerful scene without seeming to partake of its cheerfulness.

Standing upon the top of the hill was a man of tall, gaunt figure, with a face somewhat austere in its expression.

His strongly-lined features, with a firm expression about the mouth, marked him for a man of no common mould.

He appeared to be about sixty.

As his keen grey eyes wandered over the fields below, there was a cold, determined light in them which betrayed no pleasant train of thought.

It spoke of covetous ambition.

Behind him, upon the hill top, of table shape, were poles standing up out of the earth.

Around them the sward was trampled, and the scorched grass, worn in many directions into paths, signified that at no distant period the place had been inhabited.

The sign could not be mistaken; it was the site of an Indian encampment.

Elias Rody, as he turned from gazing on the panoramic view beneath, cast a glance of strange significance at these vestiges of the red man's habitation.

His features assumed a sharper cast, while a cloud came over his face.

" But for them," he muttered, " my wishes would be accomplished, my desires fulfilled."

What were his wishes?

What his desires?

Ask the covetous man such a question, and, if he answered truly, his answer would tell a tale of selfish aspirations.

He would envy youth its brightness, old age its wisdom, virtue its content, love its joys, aye, even Heaven itself its rewards, and yet, in the narrow bigotry of egotism, think he only claimed his own.

Elias Rody was a covetous man, and such were the thoughts at that moment in his mind.

They were too bitter for silence, and vented themselves in words, which the winds alone listened to.

"Why should these redskins possess what I so deeply long for; and only for their short temporary enjoyment? I would be fair with them; but they wrap themselves up in their selfish obstinacy, and scorn my offers."

How selfish others appear to a selfish man.

"Why should they continue to restrain me? If gold is worth anything, surely it should repay them for what can be only a mere fancy. I shall try Oluski once again, and if he refuse——"

Here the speaker paused.

For some time he stood in contemplation, his eye roving over the distant view.

As it again lighted upon the settlement, a smile, not a pleasant one, curled his lip.

"Well, there is time yet," said he, as if concluding an argument with himself. "I will once more try the golden bribe. I will use caution; but here will I build my house, come what may."

This natural conclusion, to an egotistic mind, appeared satisfactory.

It seemed to soothe him, for he strode down the hill with a springy, elastic step, more like that of a young man than one over whose head had passed sixty eventful years.

---

# CHAPTER III.

### ELIAS RODY.

HILE Elias Rody is pondering upon his scheme, let us tell the reader who he is.

A Georgian, who began life without any fixed idea.

His father, a wealthy merchant of Savannah, had brought him up to do nothing; and, until he had attained man's estate, he faithfully carried out his father's teaching.

Like many Southern lads born to competence, he could not appreciate the dignity of labour, and accordingly loitered through his youthful life, wasting both time and patrimony before discovering that idleness is a curse.

At his father's death, which happened upon Elias reaching his twentieth year, all the worthy merchant's property descended to the son, and the idler suddenly found himself the possessor of a large sum of money, with a sort of feeling that something was to be done with it.

He accordingly spent it.

Spent it recklessly, freely and rapidly, and then discovered that what he *had* done was not the thing he *should* have done.

He then became reformed.

Which meant, that from a liberal, open-handed, careless fellow, he changed to a cynical, cautious man.

With a small remnant of his fortune, and an inheritance from a distant relative, Elias became a man of the world, or rather, a worldly man.

In other words, he began life for a second time, and on an equally wrong basis.

Before his eyes were two classes of his equals. Reckless men with large hearts, and careful men with no hearts at all, for such was the organisation of the society surrounding him.

Of the first class he had full experience; of the second he had none whatever.

To the latter he resolved to attach himself.

It is useless wondering why this should have been. Perhaps he had never been fitted for the community of large-hearted men, and had only mixed with them through novelty, or ignorance of his own station.

Be this as it may, one thing is certain, he became before long a most exemplary member of the society he had selected for imitation. No one drove a closer bargain, saw an advantage (to himself), or could lay surer plans for securing it, than Elias Rody.

He learned, also, to control, and in every way wield influence over those around him. Power became his dream.

He was ambitious of governing men. Strange to say, this feeling was almost fatal to his prospects. We say strange, because ambition generally carves its own road, and moulds its own fortune.

Rody, however, had commenced an active career too late to arrive at much importance in the political world—that grand arena for attaining distinction.

He therefore cast about him for another field of ambitious strife, and speedily found it.

At this time throughout the State of Georgia were many planters who, without capital to purchase additional property, found themselves daily growing poorer as their land became worn out with exhausting crops.

These men were naturally enough the grumblers and discontented spirits of the community.

Another class were those with little save a restless disposition, ever ready for any venture that may arise.

Rody, shrewd and plausible, saw in these men the very instruments for a purpose he had long thought of, and had well matured.

" If I cannot attain the object of my wishes here," said he, to himself, " perhaps I may be successful elsewhere, if I can only persuade others to join me. These are men ready to my hand; I will take them with me; they shall be my followers; and whilst contributing their means to my end, they will look upon me as a benefactor."

Rody, it will be seen, was a thorough egotist.

This idea becoming fixed in his mind, the rest was easy. He spoke to them of their present condition; drew a brilliant picture of what might be achieved in a new land; painted with masterly eloquence the increase of wealth and happiness his plan presented, and finally gathered around him a large number of families, with whom he started from Georgia, and settled in that section of Florida we have described.

The reason for Rody's selection of this spot was another proof of his profound selfishness.

In his reckless, generous days, he had, on the occasion of a visit to Columbus, been the means of saving from insult and outrage a Seminole chief, who had visited the capital upon some business connected with the State government.

This act of generosity had been impulsive; but, to the Indian, it assumed the proportion of a life-long debt.

In the fulness of his gratitude, the chief caused papers and titles to be drawn up in Rody's favour, giving a grant of a portion of his own property lying on the shores of Tampa Bay.

The Indian chief was named Oluski.

The grant of land was the settlement we have spoken of.

Rody, at the time, made light of Oluski's gratitude, and thrust the titles into his desk without bestowing a second thought on the matter.

Now, in his days of worldly wisdom, these papers with the Seminole's emblematic signature, were brought to light with a very different appreciation.

He saw that they represented value.

Elias Rody accordingly determined to make use of them.

It ended in his carrying a colony southward, and settling upon Tampa Bay.

The scheme which had originated in selfishness turned out a success.

The lands were valuable, the climate salubrious, and the colony throve.

A bad man may sometimes do a good thing without intending it.

Rody received even more credit and renown than he had expected; and being a shrewd man, he achieved a part of his ambition.

He was looked up to as the most important personage in the community.

Although some of the settlers did not approve of all his measures, still, their opposition was rather negative than positive, and had, as yet, found vent only in remonstrances or grumbling.

None had dared to question his prerogative, although he often rode a high horse, and uttered his diction in a tone offensively arrogant.

What more, then, did Elias Rody want?

A covetous man always wants more.

Oluski's gift was a noble one. It covered a large area of fertile land, with water privileges, and a good harbour for trade.

It was the choicest portion of his possessions. The chief, in bestowing it, gave as a generous man gives to a friend. He gave the best he had.

Unfortunately the best he had did not embrace the hill; and therefore Rody was dissatisfied.

More than once, during the progress of the settlement, he had cast a wishful eye upon the spot, as the choicest site in the whole district for a dwelling.

As his means expanded so had his tastes, and a grand dwelling became the great desire of his life.

It must, perforce, be built upon the hill.

To every offer made to Oluski for a cession of this spot, the chief had firmly and steadfastly given a refusal.

He, too, had his ambition; which, although not so selfish as the white man's, was not a whit less cherished.

For nine months in the year Oluski and his tribe dwelt in a distant Indian town, and only visited the waters of Tampa Bay for the remaining three, and then only for purposes of pleasure.

The wigwams of himself and people were but temporarily erected upon the hill. For all this, they had an attachment for the spot; in short, they loved it.

This was what Elias Rody stigmatised as a mere fancy!

There was another reason held in similar estimation by Elias.

In the rear of their annual encampment was an Indian cemetery.

The bones of Oluski's ancestors reposed therein.

Was it strange the spot should be dear to him?

So dear was it, in fact, that to every proposal made by Rody for the purchase of the hill, Oluski only shook his head and answered " No."

---

## CHAPTER IV.

### CRIS CARROL.

MELATU recovered from his wounds.

Warren had conducted him to a hut, the temporary residence of a man of the name of Cris Carrol.

This individual was a thorough specimen of a backwoods hunter.

He was rough in manner, but in disposition gentle as a child.

He detested the formalities and restrictions of civilisation.

Even a new settlement had an oppressive air to him, which he could not endure.

It was only the necessity of disposing of his peltries and laying in a stock of

ammunition that brought him into any spot where his fellow creatures were to be found.

To Cris Carrol the sombre forest, the lonely savannah, or the trackless swamp, were the congenial homes, and bitterly he adjured the compulsory sojourn of a few days every year amongst those to whom society is a pleasure.

It was always a joyful day to him when he could shoulder his rifle, sling his game bag over his shoulder, and start anew upon his lonely explorations.

When Warren brought the wounded Indian to Carrol's rude hut, the old backwoodsman accepted the responsibility, and set himself to the task of healing his wounds with alacrity.

Nelatu was known to him, and he was always disposed to be a friend to the red man.

"No, of course not," said he to Warren, in answer to his explanations. "I don't see as how you could take the redskin up to the governor's house. Old dad wouldn't say no, but he'd look mighty like wishin' to. No, Warren, lad, you've done the right thing this time, and no mistake, and that there's sayin' more nor I would always say. Leave the boy to me. Bless you, he'll be all right in a day or two, thanks to a good constitution, along of living like a nat'ral being, and not like one of them city fellows as must try and make 'emselves unhealthy by sleepin' in beds, and keeping warm by sittin' aside of stoves, as if dried leaves and dried sticks warn't enough for 'em."

Carrol's skill as a physician was little short of marvellous.

He compounded and prepared medicines according to unwritten prescriptions, and used the oddest materials; not alone herbs and roots, but earths and clays were laid under contribution.

A few days of this forest doctoring worked wonders in Nelatu, and before a week was over, he was able to sit at the back door of the hunter's dwelling, basking himself in the sun.

Carrol, who had been in a fever of anxiety greater even than his patient, was in high glee at this.

After giving the Indian youth a preparation to allay his thirst, he was on the point of packing up his traps to start upon one of his expeditions, when he saw an individual approaching his cabin from the front.

Thinking it was Warren Rody, he called out to him that Nelatu was all right.

He was somewhat surprised to perceive that instead of Warren, it was his father.

"Good morning, neighbour," said Elias.

"Mornin', governor."

"How is your Indian patient?" asked he whom Carrol called governor. "I hope he has entirely recovered."

"Oh, he's ready, now, for the matter of that, to stan' another tussle, and take another thrust. It wasn't much of a wound arter all."

"Oh, indeed," said Elias; "I heard from my son Warren that it was a bad one."

"Perhaps your son ain't used to sich sights; there's a good deal in that. Would you like to see the Injun? He's outside, at the back."

"No, thank you, Carrol; I didn't come to see him, but you. Are you busy?"

"Well, not so busy but I can talk a spell to you, governor, if you wishes it. I war only packin' up a few things ready for a start to-morrow."

Saying this, Carrol handed the governor a stool—the furniture of his hut not boasting of a chair.

"And so you're off to-morrow, are you?"

"Yes, I can't stand this here idle life any longer than I'm obleeged; 'taint my sort. Give me the woods and the savanners."

At the very thought of returning to

"'SANSUTA, YOUR COUSIN, WACORA, STANDS BEFORE YOU.'"

them, the backwoodsman smacked his lips.

"When did you see Oluski last?" abruptly asked Elias.

"It war a fortnight ago, governor, near as my memory sarves me, just arter I'd shot the fattest buck killed this season. Oluski's people war all in a state o' excitement at the time."

"Indeed; about what?"

"Wal, Oluski's brother, who war chief o' another tribe, died not long 'fore, and his son, Wacora, had succeeded to the chiefship. Oluski was mighty perlite to his nephy, who war on a visit to Oluski's town when I war thar. I expect they'll all be hyar soon. It's about thar time o' comin' to Tampa."

"Did you see this Wacora, as you call him?"

"I did so, governor," answered Carrol, "and a likely Injun he is."

Elias sat for some moments silent, during which time Cris busied himself over his gun.

After a time he put the question—

"Is that all you ha' to say, governor?"

The governor, as Carrol styled him, started at this abrupt interrogatory.

"No, Carrol, that is not all. What I have to say is this. You are a friend to the redskins?"

"Yes, siree, so long as they behave themselves, I am," promptly replied Cris.

"I also am their friend," said Rody, "and want to deal fairly by them. They have, however, a foolish sort of pride that makes it difficult, especially in some matters. You know what I mean, do you not?"

"Yes, I see," rejoined the hunter, in a careless drawl.

"Well, in a bit of business I have with Oluski, I thought a friend might manage with him better than I could myself."

The governor paused to give Carrol an opportunity of replying to his vague suggestions.

The backwoodsman, however, did not avail himself of it.

"So, you see, Carrol," continued Elias, "I thought that you might act the part of that friend in the negociation I allude to."

"No, I don't quite see *that*," said Cris, looking up with an odd smile upon his face, and a twinkle in his eye. "But come, governor, tell me what you want done, and I'll tell you whether I kin do it."

"Well, then, Carrol, I will."

The governor drew his stool nearer to Cris, as if about to impart some confidential secret.

# CHAPTER V.

### PLAIN SPEECH.

HE backwoodsman preserved a wary look, as if suspicious of an attempt to corrupt him.

He was not alarmed. Cris Carrol knew himself to be incorruptible.

"Well, Mr. Carrol," proceeded the governor, after a pause, "you know that my settlement has prospered, and, as you may imagine, I have made money along with the rest."

"Yes, I know that," was the curt answer.

"And, having now got a little ahead of the world, I feel that I have a right to indulge some of my fancies. I want a better house, for instance."

"Do you now?" said Cris.

"And so I've made up my mind to build; and I want a good site. Now you see what I am driving at."

"Well, no; I can't say that I do exactly."

"Why, Cris, you are dull to-day. I say I want a good site for my new house."

"Well, ain't you got hundreds of acres—enough and to spare for the most tremenjous big house as was ever built?"

"That's true; but on all my land there's not a spot I really like. Does that seem strange to you?"

"Mighty strange to me, but perhaps not so strange to you, governor."

"But there *is* a bit of ground, Cris," continued Elias, "that I do like exceedingly. The worst of it is, it's not mine."

"Why don't you buy it?"

"Just what I wish to do; but the owner won't sell."

"Perhaps you don't offer enough."

"No, that's not the reason."

"What is it, then?"

"Do you know the top of the hill?" abruptly asked Rody.

"What, where the Injuns make their camp?"

"Yes; that's the place where I want to build. Oluski won't sell that piece of property to me—why, I don't know."

The governor did not stick very closely to the truth while talking on matters of business.

"Wal, what have I to do with that?" asked the backwoodsman.

"Why, I thought if you were to see Oluski, perhaps you might talk him into letting me have the ground. I've set my mind on it; and I wouldn't care if it cost me a good round sum. I'll pay you well for any trouble you may take in helping me."

Elias Rody had but one estimation of his fellow man, and that was, that every one has his price.

In the present instance he was mistaken.

"It won't do, governor, it won't do," said Carrol, shaking his head. "I see, how, plain as can be, what you're after. But I won't help you in it. If you wants the property, and Oluski won't let you have it, then the Injun's got his own reasons, and it ain't for me to try and change 'em. Besides," added he, "I don't like the job; so no offence meant, but I must say no—and I says it once and for all. Is that all you've got to say to me?"

The governor bit his lips with vexation, but, possessing a wonderful command over his temper, he merely inquired what his son had said about Nelatu.

"Well, sir, he didn't say much about anything special, except to ask me to look after the Injun lad, and see to his wounds; I did that in first-class style. And as I told you afore, *he's* all right. Your son has been every day to see my patient, as the doctor chaps calls them they physics. He 'peared mighty anxious to know how it was that he had come over to this part of the country alone, and where was the young girl, his sister."

"Ah! so he was inquiring about her, was he?" exclaimed Rody, rising and pacing the hut with restless steps. He was glad of a pretext for his rage.

The backwoodsman uttered a prolonged whistle.

Suddenly pausing in his impatient strides, the governor faced towards him.

"So he was anxious about her, was he?"

Elias Rody was evidently out of temper, and not now afraid to show it.

But Carrol was not exactly the person to care much about this.

"He was," was his cool answer; "but I don't know how I've got anything to do with it, except to tell him and you, too, for the matter of that, that the red man has his rights and feelings. Yes, and they're both worth considerin' as much as if they war pale-faces like ourselves."

"And why to me, sir?" asked the governor.

"Well, just because I ain't afraid to say to your face what I'd say behind your back, and that is, that your son had better stop thinking about that gurl, Sansuta, as soon as may be, and that you'd best see to it afore worse happens."

A very outspoken man was the backwoodsman, and Elias Rody was sorry now for having visited him.

Before he could recover from his surprise, Carrol resumed speech.

"There ain't no good, governor, in mincing matters. Last year, when Oluski war here, your son war always prowlin' 'bout the Injun encampment, and down in the grove whar the gurl used to be. He war always a talkin' to the chief's darter, and making presents to her. I know what I seed, and it warn't jest the thing."

"Perfectly natural, man," said the governor, mastering his chagrin, and speaking calmly; "perfectly natural all that, seeing that Nelatu, Sansuta, and my son, grew up as children together."

"All that may be, but it ain't no use applyin' it now that they're most growed up to be man and woman, and you knows it, governor, as well as I do; as for Nelatu, he don't amount to shucks; and I sometimes wonder whether he is Oluski's son after all."

The home truth in the first part of Carrol's speech pleased the " governor " as little as any of his previous remarks, and surprised at the freedom of the backwoodsman's language, he was silent.

Not so Cris, who had evidently determined to say more. His garrulity was unusual; and once started, he was too honest to hold his peace.

" Governor, there's many things I've had in me to say to you at a convenient time. That time's come, I reckon, and I may as well clear it off my mind.

" I don't belong to y'ur colony. I'm only a 'casional visitor, but I sees and hears things as others don't seem to dare to tell you o', though why I can't fancy; for you're only a man arter all, although you air the head man o' the settlement.

" As near as I can fix it in my mind, all y'ur people hev' settled hyar on land that once belonged to the Injun. This being the case, it seems to me that the same laws as is made for the white man is made for the red-skins too.

" Now, governor, it ain't so; or, if they are made, they ain't carried out; and, when there's an advantage to be got for the white man at the expense of the Injun, why, you see the law's strained just a leetle to give it.

" It's only a leetle now, but bye and bye it'll be a good deal. I know you'll say that's only natural, too, because that's the way you think; but I tell you, Mr. Rody," here Carrol became excited, " that it *ain't* natural nohow;

and it ain't right; and therefore, mischief's sure to come o' it.

" Now, I tell *you*, because you've more brains and more money than any o' the rest, of course you've got more to answer for.

" So them's my sentiments, and you're welcome to them, whether you like 'em or no."

" Well, Mister Carrol," replied Rody, with a withering emphasis on the " Mister," " I'm glad you've given me your opinion—it's a valuable one, no doubt."

" I don't know whether it's a valuable one, but I know it's a honest one," answered Cris with a quiet dignity, that, despite his rough dress, bespoke him a gentleman.

" I have no object in giving advice to you, governor. I only feel it a duty, and I like to discharge my duties. The same way I thinks about your son Warren running after this Injun girl. No good 'll come o' that neyther."

Whatever reply the " governor " would have made to this last observation was cut short by the entrance of Warren Rody himself.

Seen now in the light of open day, the young man presented a strange contrast to his father. Of small stature, effeminate countenance, restless, shifting eyes, and a vacillating expression of mouth, he did not look like the son of the hard, rugged man who stood beside him.

He was neatly, almost foppishly dressed, and had a self-sufficient air not altogether pleasant. He seemed like one who would rather pass through the world with oily smoothness, than assert himelf with confidence of power, and honesty of purpose.

By one of those strange mental impressions impossible to account for, both Cris and the "governor" felt that Warren had been a listener.

If so, he did not betray any sign of annoyance at what he had heard, but stood smilingly tapping his boot with a handsome riding-whip.

"Ah, father, you here? Have you come to see the invalid, or to say ' good bye' to the hunter, who tells me he is off to the wilderness to-morrow ?"

His father did not answer him, but turning to Carrol, said—

"The matter I intended to have spoken to you about will do at another time; but I'm still much obliged to you for your *good* advice."

This was spoken with as much cutting politeness as could be well pressed into the speech.

As he turned to leave, he said aside to his son, " Be home early, Warren. I have something particular to say to you."

Warren nodded and his father passed out of the house, not at all pleased with the interview between himself and the backwoodsman.

Nothing disconcerts scheming men more than blunt honesty.

As soon as the governor was gone, Carrol commenced humming a song. His new visitor waited for several moments before speaking to him.

" How is Nelatu ?" he at length asked. " Will he be strong enough to travel to-morrow ?"

" Not quite," said Carrol, pausing in the chorus part of his ditty; "he'd best remain here till his people come. They won't be long now, and the stay will give him time to get right smart."

" What was it that vexed my father, Cris ?"

" Well, I don't know 'cept he's took somethin' that's disagreed with him. He *do* seem riled considerable."

" But, Cris, are you really off tomorrow?"

" By sunrise," answered Carrol.

" Which way are you going ?"

Cris looked slightly at his questioner before answering.

" I don't know for sure whether it'll be along the bay, or across the big swamp. The deer are gettin' scarce near the settlement, and I have to go further to find 'em. That's all along of civilisation !"

" If you go by the swamp, you might do me a service," said Warren.

" Might I ?" Then, after a thoughtful pause, the backwoodsman continued —" Well, you see, Warren, it won't be by the swamp. I've made my mind up now, and I'm goin' along the bay."

Warren said, " All right; no matter."

Then, with a word of explanation, parted from Cris, and proceeded to find Nelatu.

As soon as he was out of sight, Carrol's behaviour would have furnished a comic artist a capital subject for a sketch. He chuckled, winked his eyes, wagged his head, rubbed his hands, and seemed to shake all over with suppressed merriment.

" A pair of the artfullest cusses I ever comed across. Darn my pictur', if the young un ain't most too good.

War I goin' by the swamp, cos then I might do him a service?

"No, no, Mister Warren, this coon ain't to be made a cat's-paw of by you nor your father neyther. I ain't a goin' to mix myself up in either of your scrapes, leastways, not if I knows it; nor Nelatu shan't if I can help it anyhow.

"I don't let him stir till his fellow Injuns come, and, maybe, that'll keep him out o' trouble. No, Master Warren, you must do y'ur own dirty work, and so must y'ur father.

"Cris Carrol shan't help either o' you in that. If the young un don't mind what he's heard, although he made b'lieve he didn't, and his father don't mind what I told him, there'll be worse come of it."

---

## CHAPTER VI.

### CROOKLEG.

HEN young Rody took his departure from Carrol's hut, he went off in no very enviable mood.

His interview with Nelatu, although of the briefest, had been as unproductive of results as that with the blunt old backwoodsman.

The plain speaking indulged in by Carrol, and which he had overheard before entering the cabin, had annoyed him, while the oracular manner adopted by Cris in no way assuaged the feeling.

The fact of the matter is that the old hunter had made a clear guess at the truth.

Warren had a passion for Sansuta, the daughter of Oluski.

Not a manly, loving passion, though.

Her beauty had cast a spell upon him. Had his soul been pure, the spell would have worked its own cure. Out of the magic of her very simplicity would have arisen chaste love.

But his heart was wicked, and its growth weeds.

Hitherto the difference of race had shielded from harm the object of his admiration. He would have been ashamed to avow it in an honest way. Secretly, therefore, he had forged a false friendship for her brother, as a mask to conceal his base treachery.

In the incident with which our tale opens, he had found a ready means of advancing his own interests by more closely cementing Nelatu's simple friendship, and moulding it to his will.

We have said that Red Wolf, the would-be assassin, fell by the bullet of his rifle.

With his hand upon his trigger, and in the very act of sending this wretch to his account, a thought had flashed across young Rody's mind, which made his aim more certain.

Let us explain.

Nelatu said that Red Wolf had spoken wicked words of Sansuta and of Warren.

The very conjunction of their names supplied the calumny.

Nelatu spoke truly, but what he did not know was, that the wretch who paid the forfeit of his life for his foul speech was only the dupe of Nelatu's own friend, Warren Rody.

Red Wolf, an idle, drunken scamp, had been a fit instrument in Rody's hands to be employed as a messenger between him and the Indian girl.

For these services, Red Wolf received repeated compensation in gold.

But the old story of the bad master becoming discontented with a bad servant was true in this case.

Warren was afraid that Red Wolf would, in one of his drunken orgies, talk too much, and betray the secret with which he had entrusted him.

So far, he was right, for it was whilst endeavouring to warn Nelatu of his sister's danger, that Red Wolf made use of language about the girl.

He had reviled Nelatu's sister while traducing his friend.

The issue is already known.

Wicked were Warren's thoughts as he stood, rifle in hand, watching the two.

If Red Wolf—and he recognised him at once—were removed in the very act of killing Nelatu, a dangerous tongue would be for ever silenced, while Nelatu's friendship would be further secured, and Sansuta eventually become his.

The decision was taken, the bullet sent through Red Wolf's brain, and Warren Rody accomplished a part of his design.

Having succeeded so far, it was terribly mortifying to find that one clear-sighted individual had penetrated his schemes, and without appearing to do so, had placed a restraint upon the otherwise warm sense of gratitude with which Nelatu regarded him.

All this Cris Carrol had done, and, therefore, Warren Rody was angry with him.

He left the cabin, vowing vengance upon Carrol, and casting about for the means to accomplish it.

He had not long to wait, or far to seek.

At the end of the bye-road upon which the backwoodsman's dwelling stood, he encountered the very tool suitable for his purpose.

It was in the person of a negro, with a skin black as Erebus, who was seen perched upon the top of a tall fence.

He was odd enough looking to attract the attention of the most careless traveller.

His head, denuded of the old ragged piece of felt he called hat, was unusually large, and covered with an enormous shock of tightly-curling wool.

This did not, however, conceal the apish form of the skull, that bore a strong resemblance to that of a chimpanzee.

Rolling and sparkling in a field of white, were eyes preternaturally large, and wickedly expressive, above a nose and mouth of the strongest African type.

His arms were ludicrously long, and seemed by their unusual proportions to make up for the shortness and impish form of the body.

He was whistling in a discordant strain some wild melody, and kicking his heels about like one possessed.

As Warren Rody approached, he paused in his ear-splitting music, and leaped nimbly from his perch, whilst flourishing his tattered felt in a sort of salutation.

It might have been observed that he was lame, and the few halting steps he took imparted a droll, hobbling motion to his diminutive body.

His dress was a curious warp of rags, woven, as it were, upon a still more ragged woof.

They were held together more by sympathy than cohesion.

In his right hand was a stout gnarled stick, with which he assisted himself in his frog-like progress.

At sight of young Rody, the huge mouth of this uncouth creature seemed to open from ear to ear.

"Ha, ha! Whoo, whoo! Gor bress me, if it ain't Massa Warren hisself dat I see! My stars, massa, but dis ole man am glad to see ye, dat he is!"

Such was his salutation.

The young man came to a stop, and surveyed the negro with a smile.

"Well, Crookleg, what do you want with me, you old fiend?"

"Ha, ha! Ho, ho! Bress him, what a brave young gen'lman it is! How han'som'—jess like a pictur'. What do the old fien' want? Why, he want a good deal, massa, a good deal."

"Are you out of work again?"

"Ha, ha, ain't done a bressed stroke of work, massa, for more nor two week! Ain't, 'pon dis old nigger's solemn word! Ain't had it, massa, to do. Poor Crookleg am most used up, sa, most used up."

As if to prove his last assertion, the hideous wretch cut a high caper into the air, and settled down again in a grotesque attitude.

Young Rody laughed heartily at this feat, slapped his riding-whip roughly across the negro's back, pitched a piece of silver to him, and passed on.

Whilst Crookleg stooped to pick up the coin, he glanced after him under his arm, and saw, with some surprise, that the youth had paused at a few paces' distance as if in thought.

After a time the latter faced round and came back along the road.

"By the way, Crookleg," said he, "come up to the house; my sister may have something to give you."

"Ha, ha! he, he! Miss Alice, bress her, so she may, massa! I'll come, sartin; dis old nigger's always glad to get what he can from Miss Alice."

"And," continued Rody, "ask for me when you come. I may find something for you to do that'll help you along a little."

Not staying to hear the voluble expressions of gratitude with which Crookleg overwhelmed him, Warren rapidly strode on, and was soon lost to sight.

The moment of his disappearance the darkey perpetrated another aerial leap, and then hobbled off in a direction opposite to that pursued by the governor's son.

He could be heard muttering as he went—

"Wants to see dis chile, does he? Why, dat looks good for de old nigger; and, who knows, but what de long time am a coming to an end, and all dis old nigger's work is gwine to be done for him by odder folk. He, he! dat would make dis chile bust a laffin'! He, he, he!"

## CHAPTER VII.

### THE TWO CHIEFS.

UR story now takes us fifty miles inland from Tampa Bay.

The spot on the edge of an everglade.

The hour noon.

The dramatis personæ two Indians.

One an old man, the other in the prime of life.

The first white-headed, wrinkled, and with traces of a life spent in action.

He presented an appearance at once striking and picturesque as he stood beneath the shade of a tall palm tree.

His dress was half-Indian, half-hunter.

A buckskin shirt, leggings, and moccasins richly worked with beads; a wampum-belt crossed his shoulder; a scarlet blanket hung at his back, its folds displaying a figure which, in its youth must have been superb.

It still showed, in the broad chest and powerful limbs, almost its pristine strength.

Upon his head he wore a band of bead-work, in which were stuck three wing feathers of the war-eagle.

His face was full of dignity and calm repose.

It was Oluski, the Seminole chief.

His companion was no less remarkable.

As he lay stretched upon the ground leaning on one elbow, his face upturned towards that of the old man, a striking contrast was presented.

Like Oluski, his dress was also half-Indian, half-hunter, but more richly ornamented with bead-work, whilst a certain careful disposition of the attire seemed not inappropriate to his youth and bearing.

It was, however, in his features that the difference was chiefly apparent.

In the attitude he had assumed, a ray of sunshine, piercing a break between the trees, illumined his countenance.

Instead of the coppery colour of the Indian, his skin was of a rich olive, an unmistakable sign that white blood flowed in his veins.

He was remarkably handsome. His features were regular, well defined and admirably chiselled. His eyes were large and lustrous, overarched by a forehead that denoted the possession of intellect.

Like the old man, he wore a plume of eagle's feathers on his head, as also a wampum belt; but in lieu of a blanket, a robe made of skin of the spotted lynx was thrown over his shoulders.

Oluski was the first to speak.

"Must Wacora depart to-day?" he asked.

"At sunset I must leave you, uncle," replied the youth, who was his nephew, already spoken of as Wacora.

"And when do you return?"

"Not till you come back from Tampa Bay. I have still much to do. My father's death has placed me in a position of trust, and I must not neglect its duties."

"I and my tribe depart from this place in seven days."

"And Nelatu, where is he?" asked Wacora.

"I expected him ere this. He and Red Wolf went away together."

Oluski was ignorant of what had happened.

"They went upon a hunting excursion, and if not able to return in time, were to go on to the bay, and there await our coming."

"You still make your summer encampment upon the hill. I have not seen it since I was a boy. It is a shame, too, since our people are buried there."

"Yes; and, therefore, it is dear to you as to me."

"And yet the whites have a settlement near it. It was your gift to them, uncle, I remember that."

Wacora said this with an accent that sounded almost sneering.

The old chief answered warmly.

"Well, I owed their chief a debt of gratitude. I paid it. He is my friend."

"Friend!" said Wacora, with a bitter smile; "since when has the paleface been a friend to the red man?"

"Still unjust, Wacora. I thought you had changed. The foolish sentiments of youth should give place to the wisdom of age."

Oluski's eye brightened as he spoke. His heart swelled with noble feelings.

"I do not, will not, trust in the white man!" answered the young chief. "What has he done to our race that we should believe in him? Look at his acts, and then trust him if you can. Where are the Mohawks, the Shawnees, the Delawares, and the Narragansets? How has the white man kept faith with them?"

"All white men are not alike," responded Oluski. "A pale-face befriended me when I required aid. The deed always weighs against the word. I could not be ungrateful."

"Well, Oluski's gratitude has been proved," returned Wacora. "But let him beware of those on whom it has been bestowed."

The old chief did not answer, but stood in an attitude of thought.

Ideas, slumbering till now, were awakened by Wacora's words. An unknown feeling appeared to gain possession of him.

So contagious is mistrust.

"Uncle," continued Wacora, "all white men are the same. They make their homes in our land. When space is needed the Indian must yield to them. Your friend is a white man, and, therefore, the enemy of your race."

"'WHAT DO YOU WANT?' WAS ALL SHE COULD GASP."

## CHAPTER VIII.

### SANSUTA.

S we have said, Wacora had white blood in his veins.

His mother was a Spaniard, the daughter of a planter, who had lived near the town of St. Augustine.

Almost a child at the time of her capture, she eventually forgot her own kindred, and became devoted to the chief who had been her captor.

It ended in her becoming his wife and the mother of Wacora.

Albeit that in Wacora's veins white blood flowed, his soul was Indian, and he loved his father's people as if he had been of their purest blood.

He was a patriot of the most enthusiastic stamp.

His judgment, clear in most things, was clouded in estimating the qualities of the white race, simply because he had seen the worst phases of their character, its cupidity and selfishness.

Oluski would have answered his companion's address, but the same train of disagreeable thought that had entered his mind at the first part of Wacora's speech, held him silent.

Wacora proceeded.

"Enough, uncle. I did not intend to trouble you with my feelings; I meant only to warn you against danger, for danger exists in all dealings with the pale faces. They, as ourselves, are true to their instincts, and those instincts blind them to justice. Your friend, the White Chief, may be all you think of him. If so, he will rather admire your caution than blame you for mistrust; natural, because not causeless."

Whatever reply Oluski intended was postponed by the arrival of a third person, at whose coming Wacora sprang from the ground with a gesture of surprise and admiration.

The new-comer was an Indian maiden. A perfect wood nymph!

She was a girl of slight stature, beautifully-rounded limbs, with hands and feet unusually small.

Her dress was simplicity itself, yet so gracefully worn that it seemed the result of laboured art.

A tunic of bright-coloured cloth, clasped round her neck by a silver brooch, descended to her ankles, while around her waist was twisted a scarf of many colours; over her shoulders fell a bright cloth mantle, bordered with shells worked into delicate patterns; upon her head was a beadwork cap, trimmed with plumes of the white eagle, like a fringe of newly-fallen snow; her wrists were encircled with bead bracelets, whilst embroidered moccasins covered her small feet.

She smilingly approached Oluski and nestled close to the old chief.

Wacora seemed puzzled by the fair presence.

"I had forgotten," said Oluski, "that you are strangers to each other. Sansuta, your cousin, Wacora, stands before you."

Sansuta—for she it was—smiled upon the young Indian.

He did not approach the spot where the father and daughter stood.

His impassioned eloquence had vanished.

He could scarce find words for the simplest salutation.

Oluski, perceiving his bashfulness, hastened to his relief.

"Sansuta has been upon a visit, and has only now returned. It is many years since you have seen her, Wacora. You did not expect her to have grown so tall?"

Wacora finished the sentence.

"Nor so beautiful!" he said.

Sansuta cast down her eyes.

"No praise like that should reach an Indian maiden's ear," said Oluski, with a smile; "nevertheless, Sansuta is as the Great Spirit made her, that is sufficient."

The girl did not seem to share her father's sentiments; a slight pout of her beautiful lips implied that the compliment was by no means unpleasant.

Wacora was again dumb, as if half regretting what he had said.

Such is the power that beauty exercises over bravery!

The young Indian warrior actually blushed at his boldness.

"But what brings you here, Sansuta?" asked her father. "Did you not know that your cousin and myself were in council?"

The pretty Sansuta had recovered her composure.

The pout had disappeared from her lips, which, opening to answer her father's question, revealed two rows of teeth of a dazzling whiteness.

"I am here to bid you both to the evening meal," she said.

Her voice, melodious and soft, struck upon Wacora's ear like the music of the mocking bird.

The charm was complete.

Forgetful of his late conversation, forgetful for a time of his thoughts and aspirations, oblivious of his enthusiasm, he stood a very child, eagerly watching her and listening for those tones again.

It was Oluski, however, who spoke.

"Come, Wacora, let us go with her."

The old chief strode away from the spot, Sansuta by his side.

Wacora followed with a new feeling in his heart. It was love!

# CHAPTER IX.

### THE INDIAN VILLAGE.

 WEEK later the table top of the hill overlooking the settlement presented a changed picture. It was one of active life.

The naked poles formerly standing there had disappeared, and comfortable Indian dwellings—wigwams—were in their place.

At the doors of several were planted lances and spears, with plumes and pennons depending from them.

These were the residences of the chiefs.

In the centre of the group was a large building, which was carefully, almost elaborately constructed, and which far overtopped the others.

It was the council-house of the tribe.

Around the doors of their respective dwellings, the owners might be seen engaged in every variety of employment or peaceful idleness.

Children frolicked in the presence of their parents, and dusky maidens, in twos and threes, loitered up and down the main street or avenue.

At one of the doors an interesting group seemed rapt in attention at the recital of a story that was being told by an aged chief.

The chief was Oluski, and among the individuals around was his daughter, Sansuta.

The others were his kindred.

They had assembled, as was their usual evening custom, in front of his wigwam to listen to tales of virtue or valour; of deeds done by their ancestors in the days of the early Spanish settlers.

The Indians are admirable listeners, and, in the easy natural attitudes into which they fell as they leant forward to catch Oluski's words, they formed a charming tableau.

The venerable chief, with dignified action, measured speech, and great skill in modulating his voice, held their attention as much by the manner as the matter of his narrative.

As the incident he was relating developed pathos, chivalry, horror or revenge, so did his audience yield themselves to its influences.

By turns they lowered their eyes, shuddered, stared wildly around with knit brows and clenched hands.

Like all people constantly communing with nature, they were easily moved to joy or sorrow; and not civilized enough to make any attempt at concealing it.

As Oluski sat in their midst, the observed of all observers, he looked the picture of a patriarch.

The time and place were both in harmony with the subject.

Oluski's story drew to a close.

His hero had achieved his triumph.

The distressed Seminole maiden was rescued, and joy and union wound up the tale, which had for more than an hour held his listeners enthralled.

"So now, children, away! The sun is sinking in the west; the hour of council is at hand, and I must leave you. Return to-morrow, and I will relate to you some other episode in the history of our tribe."

The young people rose at the chief's bidding, and with "thanks" and "good-nights," prepared to depart, Sansuta among the rest.

"Where are you going, child?" asked her father.

"Only to the spring, father. I shall be back soon."

As the girl said this, she turned, as if wishing to avoid her father's gaze.

The other people had all departed.

"Well," said the old man, after a pause, "do not forget to return soon. I would not have you abroad after night-fall."

She murmured a few words, and sauntered away from the spot.

Oluski did not immediately depart, but stood leaning against a spear that stood up in front of his dwelling.

The old man's eyes were filled with tears, while a hand was laid upon his heart.

"Poor girl," he reflected, as he watched her form disappearing in the fast darkening twilight, "she never knew her mother. I sometimes think I have been but a poor guardian of Sansuta's steps. But the Great Spirit knows I have tried to do my duty."

Sighing heavily, he brushed the tears from his eyes, and strode off to the council-house.

# CHAPTER X.

### AN APPOINTMENT KEPT BY DEPUTY.

ET us follow the footsteps of Sansuta. Once out of sight, and conscious that she had eluded her father's observation, she quickened her steps, not in the direction of the spring, but towards a thick clump of live oaks which grew at the foot of the hill.

As she approached the spot, her pace gradually became slower, until she at length came to a stop.

As she paused, a shiver ran through her frame.

She was evidently in doubt as to the propriety of what she was doing.

The sun had sunk below the horizon, and darkness was rapidly falling over the landscape.

A distant murmuring alone gave token of the proximity of the Indian village upon the hill.

After a few moments, and while Sansuta still stood beside the grove, these sounds ceased, and perfect silence reigned around the spot.

Presently a cuckoo's note was heard—followed by another nearer and louder—that in its turn succeeded by three others.

Whilst the echo of the last still vibrated on the evening air, the maiden was startled by a sudden apparition.

It sprang into view at her very feet, as if the ground had opened suddenly to give it passage.

When the girl regained courage sufficient to look upon it, her fears were in no way lessened.

Standing in a grotesque attitude, she beheld a negro, with arms enveloped in a ragged garment, moving about like the sails of a windmill, whilst a low chuckle proceeded from his huge mouth.

"He, ho, ho! brest if de ole nigga didn't skear de galumpious Injun. He! he! he! he! gorry if de Injun beauty ain't turn white at de show of dis chile!"

It was Crookleg who spoke.

He seemed to enjoy the fright he had given the maiden; for, after having ceased to speak, his gurgling cachinnation was continued.

It was some time before Sansuta recovered presence of mind sufficient to speak to the black deformity before her.

"What do you want?" was all she could gasp.

"Ha, ha, ha! It warn't dis ugly ole nigga what the big chief's chile 'spected to meet—war it? No, I know it warn't. But don't be skeard, ole Crookleg won't hurt ye. He's as innercent as a angel. He, he, he! as a angel!"

Here another caper, similar to the

one with which he had introduced himself, placed him in a still more impish attitude.

The Indian girl had by this recovered from her first surprise, seeing that some attributes of humanity appertained to her strange interlocutor.

"Again, what do you want? Let me pass. I must return to the village."

"Gorry, an' it arn't Crookleg dat will hinder you," the negro answered, standing directly in her path. "He only want say a word to you—dat is, if you is de beautiful Sansuta, de darter of de chief?"

"I am the chief's daughter; that is my name. I am Sansuta!"

"Den de young gen'l'm'n tole dis ole darkey true when he say I find you down by de live oak grove at sunset—he tole de ole nigga true."

A blush overspread the girl's face as Crookleg spoke.

She did not answer him.

"He say to me," continued the negro, "dat I war to tell de lady," here he chuckled, "dat he, de gen'l'm'n, couldn't come to meet her to-night, on accoun' o' de ole man his bossy wot hab gib him somethin' 'tickler to do. He send ole Crookleg to tell her dat, and gib her sometin' what I've got hyar in my pocket, he! he! he!"

Saying these words, the monster made a series of movements, having in view the discovery of his pocket.

After a most elaborate and vigorous search for its aperture among the multitudinous rags, he succeeded in finding it.

Then, plunging his long right arm therein up to the elbow, he drew forth a small parcel wrapped in white paper, and tied with a string of dazzling beads.

With another acrobatic bound, he handed it to the trembling girl.

"Dere it am, safe and soun'. Dis ole nigga nebba lose nuffin, and offen find a good deal. Dat, says de gen'l'm'n, is for de most lubbly of her seck, de Missy Sansuta."

The tender look accompanying this speech was something hideous to behold.

Sansuta hesitated before taking the parcel from him, as if in doubt whether she should not decline it.

"Da! take it," he urged; "'tain't nuffin as'll go off and hurt ye; dis nigga kin swar to dat!"

Not so much this friendly assurance as a resolution the girl had come to, decided her.

She stretched forth her hand and took the package.

This done, she essayed once more to move past the negro in order to return to the hill.

Crookleg, however, still blocking up the path, made no movement to give way to her.

He had evidently something more to say.

"Lookee hyar," he continued. "I war bid to tell de lubbly Injun lady that the gen'l'm'n wud be at dis berry spot to-morrow mornin' early to meet her, and I war 'tickler told say dat it war private, and not to be told to no 'quisitive folks wat might want to know. Now I think," here Crookleg took off his tattered hat and scratched his wool, "yes, dat's all dis nigga was tole to say—yes, dat's all."

Without waiting for a reply, the monstrosity made a pirouette, then a bound, and disappeared so suddenly, that he was gone before Sansuta could recover from her surprise.

Once assured that she was alone, the maiden hastened to untie the bead-string around the packet, and bare its contents.

Her glance fell upon a pair of showy ear-rings, and affixed to them a small slip of paper.

Though but an Indian maiden, the chief's daughter had learned to read.

By the last glimpse of departing twilight she read what was on the paper.

There were but two words written on it—

" From Warren."

## CHAPTER XI.

### THE COUNCIL.

LUSKI'S entrance into the council-house was the signal for all eyes to turn towards him.

Slowly and with dignity he traversed the space between the door and the seat reserved for him, at the upper end of the hall.

Once there, he turned around, bowed gravely to the assembled warriors, and then took his seat.

Pipes were now lighted, and gourds filled with honey and water handed around.

Oluski declined the latter, but lighted one of the pipes, and for some time watched, as if in reverie, the circling of the smoke.

The silence that ensued upon the old chief's entrance continued for several minutes.

At length a young warrior opposite to him rose and spoke—

" Will our chief tell his brothers why they are called together, and what is it that makes him thoughtful and silent ? We will hear and advise—let Oluski speak !"

After this brief address, the young man resumed his seat, whilst those around the circle murmured their assent to what he had said. Thus solicited, Oluski arose, and spoke as follows :—

" It is not unknown to many of our warriors now present that I was deputed by their elder brothers and themselves many years since to go to the palefaces in Georgia to settle some old disputes about lands sold by our people to them, and about which wicked men of both races had caused quarrels and bloodshed. I departed on my errand, went to the great town where their council-house stands, spoke truth, and made new treaties with them. All this I did, and our people were pleased !"

A chorus of voices ratified the chief's statement.

"It may be remembered that I made new friends with some of the palefaces, and concluded treaties founded on justice, which gave to our people property they needed in exchange for lands which we did not require."

Renewed signals of assent.

"To one paleface more than to others I was under bonds of gratitude. He did me great service when I required it, and I promised to repay him. An Indian chief never breaks his word. I gave to that man some of the lands left to me by my fathers. These are the lands upon which the white settlement now stands. The paleface I now speak of was Elias Rody!"

The voices of the assembled warriors were silent.

An eager look of expectancy was all the answer Oluski received at the mention of Rody's name.

The old chief continued.

"To-day, Elias Rody came here and talked with me. He told me that the hour had arrived when I could do him a great service, and again prove myself grateful for the aid he had afforded me. I told him to speak out. He did so. I listened. He said the colony he had founded was prosperous, but there was one thing he still desired; and this was the favour he came to ask. Twice before he had spoken of it. This time he required a final answer. His demand was more than I could of myself grant. I told him so. For this reason have I called you into council. I will lay his wish before you. It is for you to decide."

Oluski paused to give opportunity for any one who chose to make a remark.

None was made, but the listeners looked around them as if trying to read each other's thoughts.

The chief proceeded.

"What the white man wants is to buy from us this hill upon which our habitations are built."

A chorus of angry, dissentient voices greeted the proposal.

"Hear me out," continued Oluski, "and then decide."

Silence ensued as sudden as the noisy interruption.

"The white chief offered me one hundred rifles, two hundred square Machinaw blankets, five kegs of gunpowder, fifteen bales of cloth, and one hundred shot belts, besides beads, knives and small articles.

"For this he desires to have possession of the hill as far as the borders of the settlement, and the strip of land lying along the shore of the bay.

"I have told you this with no remark of my own to influence your decision. To you, brothers, I leave it. Whatever it may be, Oluski will abide by it."

Saying this, he sat down.

The young warrior who had already spoken, once more rose to his feet, and addressed himself to the chief.

"Why does Oluski ask us to decide? The land is his, not ours."

Without rising, the chief replied to the question.

His voice was sad and subdued, as though he were speaking under compulsion.

"I have asked you, my sons," said

he, "for good reason. Although the land is my own, the graveyard of our ancestors, which adjoins the property, belongs not only to the whole tribe, but to the children of the tribe for ever!"

A silence, such as precedes a storm, fell upon the assembly.

Then every voice within the council chamber was simultaneously raised in loud protestations, and had Elias Rody seen the flashing eyes and angry gestures, or heard the fierce invectives hurled back to his proposal, he would have hesitated to renew it.

Amidst the wild tumult Oluski sate, with head bowed upon his breast, a feeling of sorrow in his heart.

The angry debate that succeeded did not last long; it was but the ebullition of a common sentiment, to which the expression by one voice was alone wanting.

It found it in the same youthful warrior who had spoken before.

The feelings of the warriors being known, he, as well as any other, could give them voice.

"The chosen of the tribe have decided," said he amidst perfect silence; "I will proclaim their answer."

"Do so," Oluski said, simply raising his head.

"They despise the white chief's bribe offered for the bones of our ancestors. They bid me ask Oluski what answer he intends making to the paleface."

The old chief rose hastily to his feet, his form and eyes dilated.

Glancing proudly around the assembly, he cried out, in a clear, ringing voice—

"Oluski's answer is written here."

As he said this, he struck his spread palm upon his breast.

"When the white chief would have it, it shall be NO!"

A cry of approbation from every warrior present greeted this patriotic speech.

Hastening forward, they pressed around their chief with ejaculations of joy.

The aged patriarch felt his blood freshly warmed within his veins—he was young again!

In a few moments the excitement subsided, and the warriors, returning from the council-house, moved off towards their respective dwellings.

Oluski was the last to emerge from the council-chamber.

As he stepped across the threshold, the fire that had animated him seemed to have become suddenly extinguished.

His form was bent, his steps tottering and listless.

As he looked down the hill, he caught a glimpse of the white settlement, with its window-lights twinkling through the darkness.

One, more brilliant than the rest, attracted his attention.

It was the house of Elias Rody.

"I fear," said the old chief, in a dreamy voice, "my gift will prove fatal alike to him and me. When ambition enters the heart, honour and justice find no home therein. Our people cannot know that man in the past; they must judge him by his present. I would be generous—the Great Spirit knows that—but I must also be just. If I have raised angry feelings at this council, I have nothing to charge myself with; I but did my duty. May the White Chief's heart be turned from the covetous thoughts which fill it! Great Spirit, hear my prayer!"

With a natural and beautiful action, the aged Indian raised his hands in supplication to that Power alike cognizant of the thoughts of white and red.

---

## CHAPTER XII.

### THE SITUATION.

SEVERAL days had elapsed since the meeting in the council-house.

The answer of the Seminole warriors had been conveyed to the white governor by Oluski himself.

The old chief couched the decision in kindly words mingled with regrets.

Elias Rody was wonderfully self-possessed.

He smiled, shrugged his shoulders, grasped the Seminole's hand, and with a wave of his own, seemed to dismiss the subject from his thoughts.

Nay, more, he presented the old warrior with a beautifully inlaid rifle, a bale of broadcloth, and a keg of powder.

" Come, come," said he, speaking in the friendliest tone, " don't let a mere whim of mine affect such a friendship as ours. You must accept these things—mere trifles. Your taking them will prove that you harbour no unkindness towards me or mine."

Thus pressed, Oluski accepted the presents.

The governor smiled covertly as the old chief departed.

\* \* \* \* \*

Nelatu had recovered from his wound; he daily spent hours in company with Warren, and there was no lack of diversion for the white youth or his redskinned companion.

Their canoe darted through the blue waters of the bay, or stole dreamily along the river's current.

Their rifles brought down the wildfowl upon the sea, or the quail and partridge upon the land.

Their fishing rods and spears furnished many a dainty dish.

Sometimes, going farther afield, they would bring home a deer, or a brace or two of wild turkeys—or, bent on destruction, would penetrate some dark lagoon and slay the hideous alligator.

The opportunities which these pursuits presented, were constantly improved by Warren.

He moulded his conduct and expressions to suit the simple faith and understanding of his Indian companion.

He concealed the dark thoughts that were brooding in his bosom, and was the very semblance of what he professed to be—a friend; not a shadow of the evil he meditated was perceptible.

"THE MEETING OF WARREN BODY AND SANSUTA."

Nelatu, generous and confiding, was flattered, and with the simple faith of a child he trusted his white associate.

"Ah, Nelatu," would the latter say, "if I had only the power to do what I wish, I would prove myself a true friend to the Indians. Our race are afraid to show real sympathy with them on account of old and stupid prejudices. Wait until I am in a position to prove my words, and you will see what I will do. Why, even now, I'd rather sit near you fishing, or tramp with you across the country on a hunting excursion, than spend the time amongst my own people, who cannot understand either me or my ways."

In a thousand designing ways he impressed himself on Nelatu's mind as a chivalrous, self-sacrificing fellow, worthy the love of any maiden.

Then, adroitly singing soft praises of Sansuta to the brother's pleased ear, he ensured in him a faithful ally and warm panegyrist.

Sansuta, pleased with an admiration which she never paused to question, blushed at her brother's report of Warren's good qualities.

Many articles of adornment had come into her hands, and were kept from her father's sight.

She dared not wear them, but in secret gloated over their possession as over the feelings which had prompted the gift.

Sansuta, it will be seen, was a coquette, though one through vanity, not vice.

She was innocent as a child, but inordinately vain.

She had grown up without a mother's care; had been so much thrown upon her own resources, that all her faults were those of an untrained nature.

Her heart was warm, her affection for her father and brother deep and true; but she was too prone to turn from the bright side of life, and tremble at anything with the appearance of dulness.

Differently placed, this Indian maiden might have become a heroine.

As it was, she was nothing but a frivolous child.

With a generous man, her defenceless position would have ensured her safety.

Not thus with Warren Rody.

The son did not belie his father's nature.

Crookleg had become useful to him in his scheme.

This hideous creature proved far more subservient and trustworthy than the defunct Red Wolf, for he was all obsequious obedience.

True, he sometimes glanced askance with an ugly look bent upon his young master, but the look vanished in a hideous grin whenever the latter turned towards him.

What dark mystery lay hidden in the negro's mind, no one white knew, but all, by a common impulse, gave way to him as he passed.

Children ran shrieking, and hid their faces in their mothers' aprons; the boys paused suddenly in their play as he hobbled by, while the old gossips of both sexes shook their heads and thought of the devil as he approached them!

He seemed only flattered by these signs of detestation, and chuckled with glee at the aversion he inspired.

The Indians, meanwhile, pursued their usual avocations.

The waters of Tampa Bay were dotted with their canoes.

Troops of their children frolicked on the plateau, or plucked the wild flowers that grew along the sloping sides of the river.

The women of the tribe followed their domestic duties, and the whole scene around the wigwams was one of tranquil contentment.

The white settlers were not idle either.

The fields were swelling with crops which the planters had commenced to gather in.

A goodly store of merchandize was collected upon the wharf, and several schooners had come to an anchor in the bay.

Peace and plenty abounded in the settlement.

But as, before the storm, a small, dark cloud specks the bright sky, gathering as it grows, so was there a cloud, too small for human view, drifting over this peaceful scene, which should carry death and destruction in its wake.

Slowly and surely was it coming !

---

# CHAPTER XIII.

### A SUBTERRANEAN SNARE.

 MORNING in the forest.

What beauty ! What delight !

The wild flowers gemmed with dew—the quivering foliage vieing in colour with the emerald sward—the vistas dreamily grey and endless, the air balmy, the light soft and grateful.

What a melody the birds make, a very paradise of sound !

What flashes of splendid blues, reds, and yellows, as they dart from branch to branch !

What a succession of novelties, and charms for eye and ear !

Thoughts like these filled the mind of an individual seen near the settlement on a lovely morning, a few days after the council held by Oluski with his warriors.

The individual in question was a woman.

She was on horseback, and as she checked her steed to gaze upon the scene before her, she presented to view a face and form signally beautiful.

A frank, fearless young face withal, of true maiden modesty.

Her hair, in a rich golden shower of curls, fell over a forehead of snowy whiteness, and a neck and shoulders admirably rounded.

Her figure was graceful and striking ; its contour shown off by the dark riding dress she wore.

A hat with a heron's plume, stuck saucily on one side, covered her head.

The horse she rode was a Seminole steed, of the Andalusian race, small, but well-proportioned, as evidenced by the arching of its neck, proud of its fair burden.

She remained for some time silently feasting her senses with the lovely prospect, herself a charming addition to its interest.

After awhile she gave the rein to her horse, and allowed it with a dainty, mincing step, to pick its way along the path, occasionally making a pretence of alarm, pricking up its ears, drawing its head on one side, and doubly arching its pretty neck as some idle butterfly, or quick-winged humming-bird, darted across the road, or rose suddenly from a bed of wild flowers.

For a considerable distance the young lady proceeded without adventure or mischance, whilst her horse, having apparently exhausted all its little affected airs, stepped along with an even, rapid step.

The fair equestrian's thoughts had not, it seemed, undergone any change, for the same pleasant smile illumined her countenance.

Her thoughts were gay and happy, in unison with the surroundings.

In this mood was she proceeding on her journey.

Suddenly, indeed so suddenly as to cause her alarm, her steed came to a stop, showing signs of being scared.

His eyeballs were distended, his forefeet planted stiffly in advance, his mane standing almost straight, while he trembled in every limb.

Another step, and horse and rider would have suddenly disappeared beneath the surface of the earth, and for ever.

They were on the brink of one of those subterranean wells, or "rinks," common in that part of the country, whose dangerous concavity is concealed by a light crust of earth; and only by the sudden sinking of the support beneath him is the unwary traveller apprised of the peril.

Over the covering of the abyss the grass grew as greenly, the flowers bloomed as brightly as elsewhere.

And yet under that fair seeming was a trap that conducted to death.

In an instant the fair rider comprehended her peril.

To advance would be certain death; to attempt to back her steed upon its own tracks almost as certain destruction.

She knew but one thing to do, and she did it.

Gently patting the creature's neck, she addressed it in soothing words; whilst with a wary hand she held the bridle, her touch upon the horse's mouth was so delicate that the very breeze might have swayed it.

Her hand did not tremble, nor her eye quail, although the ruddy tinge upon her cheek had altogether disappeared.

After a time the horse seemed to gain confidence; his tremor became subdued, and instead of the wild frenzy in his eye, there was a dull look, while the foam rose to his nostrils, and sweat bathed his limbs.

She continued to caress his neck, and soothe him with soft words.

Moving neither up nor down, to right nor to left, with her delicate hand she still held the bridle.

But the danger still threatened.

She saw it as she cast her eyes below.

The ground was crumbling slowly but surely beneath the horse's feet, and a fissure had already opened wide enough to show the deep, black chasm underneath.

She shuddered, closed her eyes for a second, and then opened them, onl  to see the fissure widening—the blackness growing more intense.

A prayer rose up from her lips.

She waited for the catastrophe!

The tension on the horse's nerves became too great.

Again the animal trembled!

Its knees began to yield!

The ground seemed all at once to give from beneath its feet!

His rider felt that she was lost!

No—saved!

Just as her closing eyes saw the courageous animal slide into the black chasm, and heard its last snort of terror, she felt herself lifted from the saddle, borne from the spot, and then——

She knew no more.

She had fainted!

## CHAPTER XIV.

### A TRUE GENTLEMAN.

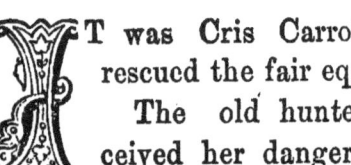T was Cris Carrol who had rescued the fair equestrian.

The old hunter had perceived her danger, and, with the quickness of thought, mastered the whole situation.

Without uttering a word, he stealthily approached the spot, until reaching a tree, one of whose branches extended over the horse's head.

To clutch it, spring out on the projecting limb, and lift the young lady out of the saddle, were acts performed almost instantaneously.

What followed was not so easy.

He had not counted on the feminine weakness of fainting, and, with the dead weight of the swooning girl upon his arm, there was still a difficulty as to his future movements. How was he to get back along the limb?

He saw that nothing but sheer strength could accomplish it, and accordingly exerted all he had.

With one hand grasping the branch, and the other round the unconscious form, he made a superhuman effort, and succeeded in reaching the trunk of the tree. Against this he supported himself until he recovered breath and strength.

While thus resting, he was witness

to the engulfing of the gallant steed, as the snorting animal sank into the chasm below.

The old hunter heaved a sigh. He was sorry for the creature, and would have saved it had the thing been possible.

"Wal, if it ain't too bad for a good, plucky crittur like that to die sich a death! Confound them tarnal sink holes! They've been the misfortun' o' many a one. Thank goodness I've saved the feminine."

The "feminine's" condition now demanded his attention, as the temporary faintness was passing away, and she showed signs of returning animation.

With rare tact and delicacy, the old hunter, regardless of his own fatigue, softly lowered himself and his fair burden to the ground. Then, gently withdrawing his arm from her waist, he drew back a step or two.

Taking off his seal-skin cap, he wiped the perspiration from his brow, and, with the gallantry of a true gentleman, waited until she should address him.

The young lady he had rescued was no ordinary person.

The faintness which had come upon her endured only for a short while.

Recovering consciousness, she understood at a glance, not only the nature of the service rendered her, but also the character of the man who had rendered it.

"Oh, sir! I'm afraid that you've run a fearful risk. I can hardly tell you how grateful I am."

"Wal, miss, it war rayther a toughish struggle while it lasted. But, bless ye, that's nothin' so long as it's turned out all right. If you'd not been the plucky one you are, nothin' I could ha' done would have helped ye. It war your own grit as much as my muscle saved ye from fallin' into that trap."

"My horse. Where is he?"

"Ye're right there, he's gone; poor crittur. I'd ha' liked to save him, too, for the way he behaved. That dumb crittur had more sense in him than many a human; and it 'ud ha' done me a sight o' good to ha' pulled him through; but it wasn't possible, nohow."

"Tell me, sir, where did you come from? I did not see you."

"Wal, I war clost by, and seed you ride right on to the danger. It war too late to holler, for that would only ha' made things worse an' skeared you both; so I said nothin', but jist dropped my rifle, and made tracks toarst ye. I spied the branch above you an' speeled up to it. The next war nothin'—only a spell o' twistin' an' wrigglin'."

He did not tell her that the muscles of his arms were fearfully swollen, and that it demanded all his power of endurance to prevent him groaning at the intense agony he suffered.

But the young lady, with a quickness of apprehension, seemed to understand this, too.

"Nothing, do you say? Oh! sir, it's another proof of your noble courage. I can never show you enough gratitude. For all that, I feel deeply grateful."

Her voice trembled with emotion—tears welled into her eyes.

Her brave heart had well endured danger, but could not contemplate, without betraying its emotion, the generosity of her preserver.

"Wal," said he, in order to change the conversation, which he thought too flattering towards himself, "what do you intend doing now that your horse is gone?"

She wiped the tears from her eyes, and in a firm voice answered him—

"I'm not more than four or five miles from my home. I merely rode out for pleasure. I little thought that my excursion would end thus. Where do you live, sir? I don't remember to have seen you before."

"At the settlement?" he asked.

She nodded.

"No; I ain't a resident of no place. I'm as you see me—a hunter. I've been at the settlement, though, many a time; in fact I used to live on that thar spot afore thar war any settlement. It war enough for me to know they war a comin', so I pulled up stakes and quit. You see, miss, it don't do for a hunter to live among the clearin's; besides, I'm a deal happier by myself."

"No doubt. To a contented mind, a life like yours must be a happy one."

"That's it, miss; to them as is contented. Do you know I've often and often puzzled over the expressin' o' that there idear, and never could hit it; and yet you've gin it in the snappin' of a jack-knife."

"Perhaps you were going to the settlement when you saw me?"

"No; exactly t'other way. I war goin' from it. I've been down beyont hyar to meet a friend o' mine. It ain't long ago, though, since I war in the colony, and stayed a spell there. Now I'm bound for the big Savanna, that is, arter I've seen you out of danger."

"Oh, no, thank you, that's not at all necessary. I'm used to wandering about alone, although this part of the country is a little new to me."

"If you'll allow me, miss, I'll go with pleasure."

"That I cannot do. All I want to know now is your name?"

"Cris Carrol," was his reply.

"Then," said she, holding out her pretty white hand, "Cris Carrol, I thank you, with my whole heart, for what you have done for me. I will remember it to my dying day."

Like a knight of ancient chivalry, the backwoodsman stooped and kissed the proffered hand.

When he stood erect again, a flush of pleasurable pride made his rugged face look as handsome as an Apollo's. It was the beauty of honesty.

"Bless you, miss, bless you! Cris Carrol will allers be too glad to do a sarvice for one that's raal grit, as you air. That I'll sw'ar to. Bless you!"

As she turned to take her departure, a sudden idea struck the backwoodsman—

"Why, what a durn'd old fool I am; I never axed her for her name."

"You'll pardon me, miss," said he, "I'm sure you will—but——"

"But what?" she asked, smilingly.

"But, might I ask you—I'd like to know——" here he stammered and stuttered.

"You want to know my name; that's it, isn't it?"

"The very thing!"

"Alice Rody."

The old backwoodsman started on hearing it.

# CHAPTER XV.

### BROTHER AND SISTER.

S Alice Rody left the spot which had so nearly proved her tomb, she thought of the old hunter with admiration. His courage and honest courtesy had won her, but she had also noticed his surprise on hearing her name.

Of the feeling entertained by him for her father and brother she knew nothing.

The female mind loves riddles, and Alice, like a true woman, racked her brain for a solution of that one Carrol's conduct seemed to embody.

Thus occupied, she emerged from the forest, and had proceeded some distance upon her road, when she perceived two individuals in close conversation.

Their backs were towards her, and as her light footfall did not disturb them, she got close to the spot on which they stood without their perceiving her.

Near enough, in fact, to hear the following—

"Hark you, you black rascal! If you betray me, it will be the worse for you. I have a means of silencing those who prove false to me."

Whatever reply the "black rascal" would have made was prevented by an impetuous gesture of the speaker, who had caught sight of Alice.

"Ah, Alice, you here?" said he, facing towards her. "I did not know you were abroad."

It was her brother Warren.

Alice recognised in the "black rascal" —no less a personage than Crookleg.

Warren thrust a piece of silver into the negro's hands.

"There, there, that'll do. I'll forgive you this time, but remember! Now be off with you—be off, I say."

Crookleg, cut short in his attempt to address Alice, hobbled away, muttering some words to himself.

"Why, Warren," asked his sister, "what makes you speak so harshly to poor Crookleg?"

"Because he's a pestilent fellow. I want him to know his place."

"But a kind word doesn't cost much."

"There, sister, no scolding, if you please. I'm not in the best of humours now. Where is your horse?"

Alice told her brother of the incident, and spoke warmly of Carrol.

"So the old hunter did you a good service, did he? I didn't think he had it in him, the old bear."

"How unjust you are, Warren. Bear,

indeed! I tell you that Cris Carrol is as good a gentleman as ever lived!"

As she said this, she showed signs of indignation.

"Is he, indeed?" was the brother's mocking retort.

"Yes—a thorough gentleman! One who wouldn't wound another's feelings if he could help it—and that's my idea of a gentleman!"

"Well, we won't argue the point. He has done good this time, and that'll go to his credit; for all that, *I* don't like him!"

Alice bit her lip with vexation, but made no reply.

"He's too officious," continued Warren; "too free with his advice—and I hate advice!"

"Most people do, especially when it is good," quickly answered his sister.

"Who said it was good?"

"I know it is, or you would have liked it, and have followed it."

"You are sarcastic."

"No—truthful."

"Well, as I am in no mood for quarrelling, we'll drop the subject, and Cris Carrol too."

"*You* may, but I shall never drop him. He is my friend from this time forward!"

"You are welcome to choose your friends—I'll select my own."

"You have done so already."

"What do you mean?"

"That Nelatu, the Indian, seems to be one of them."

"Have you anything against him?"

"Oh, no. I am only afraid he'll be the loser by the intimacy."

"Am I so dangerous?" asked her brother.

"Yes, Warren, you are dangerous, for, with all your pretended goodness, you lack principle. You cannot conceal your real character from me. Remember, I am your sister."

"I am glad you remind me. I should forget it."

"That's because you avoid me so much. If you believed in my wishes for your welfare, you would not do that."

Her voice trembled as she spoke.

"Indeed, then I beg you won't waste your sympathy on me. I'm perfectly able to take care of myself."

"You think you are."

"Well, have it that way if it pleases you better. But what has this to do with my friendship for the Indian?"

"A great deal. I don't like your intimacy with him. Not because he's an Indian—although that is one reason —but because you have some purpose to serve by it that'll do him no good."

"Why, one would think you were in love with the young copper-skin!"

"No, but they might think he's in love with me."

"What! has he dared——"

"No, he has dared nothing; only a woman's eye can see more than a man's. Nelatu has never spoken a familiar word to me, but, for all that, I can see he admires me."

"And you—do you admire him?"

The young girl stopped in her walk.

Her eyes sparkled strangely as she answered—

"Shame, brother, to put such a question! I am a white woman—he is an Indian. How dare you speak of such a thing ?"

Warren laughed lightly at his sister, as he answered—

" Why, you don't think that *I* care for the fellow, do you ?"

The young girl saw her opportunity, and seized it.

"And yet you pretend to be his friend. Ah! have I caught you by your own confession ?"

" Again, what do you mean ?"

" That my doubts are now certainties —that some wicked scheme *is* concealed under this false friendship for Nelatu."

" You are mad, Alice."

" No, perfectly sane. You have some design, and I advise you, whatever it be, to abandon it. You don't like my tears, so I'll try to suppress them if I can ; but I implore you, Warren, brother, to give it up now and for ever."

She dashed a few bitter drops from her eyes ere she spoke again.

" I have only you and my father to look to for support and comfort; my heart has yearned towards you both, but has met with nothing but coldness. Oh, Warren, be a brave man—brave enough to despise wickedness, and you will not only make me happy, but perhaps, avert that terrible retribution which overtakes transgression. There is time yet ; hear my prayer before it is too late."

Her pleading voice fell upon an ear that heard not.

The appeal did not reach her brother's stony heart.

With a few commonplaces he endeavoured to exculpate himself from any evil intentions towards the young Indian.

All in vain.

Her woman's instinct saw through his hypocrisy, and showed him to her as he was—wicked !

That night Alice Rody prayed long and earnestly for support in an affliction which she felt was but too surely coming ; and she wept till her pillow was bedewed with tears !

# CHAPTER XVI.

### A CHANGED CHARACTER.

 WONDERFUL change had taken place in the conduct of Elias Rody. He was most gracious—most condescending.

He kissed all the children, chatted with the mothers, and listened to their narratives of infant ailments, husbands' delinquencies, or household troubles.

To the surprise of many of the poorer settlers the hitherto aristocratic governor took, or appeared to take, great interest in their affairs, and, more wonderful still, in some instances, put his hand into his pocket to relieve their pressing necessities.

Petty matters seemed to become deeply interesting to him, and he devoted time and attention to their adjustment.

Through all this his temper was conciliating and amiable.

Many personal quarrels amongst settlers were forgotten and forgiven through his means, whilst coolnesses were warmed into new friendships by his mediation.

This was the work of some time, and the astonishment at his amiability gave way to self-censure on the part of the observers, who charged themselves with having done him great injustice.

No churlish man would have sent down provisions for the poor, have rebuilt Widow Jones's barn, or bought Seth Cheshire a new horse; and what mean man would have lent money to that drunken but popular Jake Stebbins? whose fiery nose, should Jake be abroad, was as a lighthouse on a dark night to any belated traveller.

This was the impression that gradually got abroad about Elias Rody.

He only smiled, rubbed his hands softly, and muttered, "Humph!"

The monosyllable was full of meaning.

It meant that he thought his labour well bestowed, and that the design he had in view prospered even beyond his expectations.

What this design was must be already apparent.

He had courted this popularity to enable him to accomplish the dearest wish of his heart.

After his bland dismissal of Oluski, laden with gifts, he had acquired a control over his own naturally impetuous temper which astonished himself.

The refusal of the Seminole chief to give him quiet possession of the hill annoyed him greatly, but the Judas smile that succeeded had root in another thought, which the governor had left out of his mind until the supreme moment of his defeat.

"WACORA AND CROOKLEG."

Hence his changed conduct towards his fellow settlers.

They became almost to a man believers in him, and ready to do his bidding.

He did not neglect, in his Machiavelian policy, to insinuate in every artful way his pet project of possessing the property on which the Indians were encamped. So artfully, indeed, that in most instances the idea seemed to have originated in his listener's mind, and by them to have been suggested to Elias, thus skilfully reversing the true facts of the case.

This once accomplished, the rest was simple.

A general feeling got abroad that the red men were interlopers, and had no right to usurp a spot so necessary and so useful to the colonists. This feeling, although not loudly expressed, was very deep, and in nearly every instance, sincere.

The few clear-headed and impartial planters who, proof against Rody's sophistical speeches, were assailed by him in a different manner—by specious promises of enlarged possessions, or by matter of fact appeals for the advancement of civilization. If he did not gain their approval, he, at any rate, made their objections seem narrow-minded and selfish.

Only a few sturdy, honest men held out. These Elias could do nothing with. They rejected his proposals, laid bare his false arguments, and laughed at his facts—but as they were a very small minority, they had little influence.

Ere Rody had accomplished this pacific revolution of opinion, the autumn had waned, and the winter months—if such a word can be used where there is no winter—approached, and with it the limit of the term of the Indians' stay upon the hill.

With the first appearance of cool weather, Oluski and his tribe repacked their household gods, took their dwellings to pieces, and with their wives, children, horses and cattle, quitted their late encampment.

The bare poles again appeared cutting against the clear sky.

The hill was once more uninhabited.

A new sort of activity had sprung into existence upon its table top.

In the place of Indians, with their painted plumes and primitive finery, the ground was occupied by white men —carpenters and other artizans, along with their negro attendants.

Piles of prepared lumber, stones and other building materials strewed the ground, whilst the busy workmen, black and white, made the air resonant with their jocund voices.

A finished frame-house soon made its appearance on the spot where the Indians had but recently dwelt—a large structure, substantially built, and ornamental in finish.

It belonged to Elias Rody.

He had secured the sanction of the settlers, and they had determined to support him in his piratical design. Only a very few of them had stood out against it.

Thus strengthened, he had resolved upon, and had now completed his act of usurpation.

## CHAPTER XVII.

### OVER CONFIDENCE.

 LUSKI'S dwelling, in his place of permanent abode, was a more pretentious affair than the wigwam temporarily inhabited by him at Tampa Bay.

This eastern residence was an old Indian town that had been built long before the Spaniards had landed in Florida, and in it his people, for many generations, had dwelt.

The chief, having returned from an extended hunting excursion, was pleased to find himself once more beneath his paternal roof.

Doubly pleased ; for he had brought back with him his nephew, Wacora, who, thinking of his pretty cousin, had accepted his uncle's invitation with alacrity.

Behold them, then, with pipes lighted, seated inside the house, Sansuta in attendance.

Wacora watched the lithe-limbed maiden ; as she flitted to and fro, engaged in household duties, he thought her as attractive as ever. A certain consciousness on her part of the fact in no way detracted from her beauty.

" I am pleased, nephew," said Oluski, " pleased to see you here again. I feel that I am no longer young ; the support of your arm in a wearying day's march has been very welcome."

" It is always at your service, uncle."

" I am sure of it. If Oluski thought otherwise, he would be unhappy. Your cousin, Sansuta," addressing his daughter, " came to see you as much as to bear me company. You should thank him for it."

" I do."

" Wacora is thanked already in the smile of welcome that met him in Sansuta's eyes."

The young girl blushed at the delicate compliment, and, going out, left the two chiefs together.

" You tell me, Wacora, that the affairs of your tribe are prosperous, and that there is peace and harmony in your council chamber ?"

" Yes, uncle, the same as in my father's lifetime."

" That is well, for without that there is no real strength. So it is with us."

" You have told me nothing of the pale-faces on Tampa Bay."

" They are our firm friends still. In spite of your fears, Wacora, to the contrary, Rody and the colonists are true to their promises."

" I am pleased to hear Oluski say so," was the nephew's reply.

"I did not tell you that he had made an offer to buy the hill."

"To buy the hill! What hill?"

"That on which we make our annual encampment. We call it Tampa after the bay."

"Indeed! He wants that too?" rejoined the young chief, in a tone savouring of indignation.

"Yes; I called our council together, and told them of the offer."

"And their answer?"

"The same as my own; they refused."

Wacora gave a sigh of relief.

"When I carried that answer to the white, he was not angry, but met me like a friend."

"Indeed!"

"Yes; he pressed upon my acceptance rich presents, and told me that Oluski's friendship was worth more than land."

"But you refused the presents?" said the young Indian, eagerly.

"I could not; my old friend would take no denial. Fearing to offend him, I yielded."

The conversation was interrupted by the entrance of an Indian, one of the warriors of the tribe.

"What does Maracota want?" asked Oluski.

"To speak to Wacora, the chief."

Wacora desired him to express his wishes in the presence of his uncle.

"Maracota must speak to Wacora alone, if Oluski will allow it."

Oluski made a sign to his nephew who, rising, followed the man outside the door.

"Wacora must follow me further," signified the Indian.

"Go on, I will do so."

Maracota led the way, and only paused in his walk when he had got some distance from the dwelling.

"Has Wacora faith in Maracota?"

The young chief started at the question which his guide had put to him in a tone of strange earnestness.

"Yes. I have faith in you."

"And he would serve Oluski, our chief?"

"With my life!"

"Sansuta is dear to Oluski."

Again Wacora started. Maracota's words were enigmatical.

His guide continued—

"Sansuta is beautiful."

"We all know that. Was it to tell me this you brought me here?"

"The pale-faces admire the beauty of our Indian maidens."

"What of that?"

"One pale-face has marked Sansuta's beauty."

"Ha!"

"His eyes gladden at sight of her. Her cheeks grow red at sight of him."

"His name?"

"Warren Rody."

"How do you know all this?"

"Maracota is Oluski's friend and watches over his chief's happiness. To-night Warren's messenger was in the town—the negro, Crookleg."

The young chief was silent. Maracota watched him without breaking in upon his thoughts.

Recovering himself, Wacora asked—

"Where did you see the negro?"

"In the old fort."

"The old fort! What was he doing there?"

"Maracota followed his trail—a lame

foot and a stick---and saw him as he entered the ruin ; some one was waiting for him inside !"

" Who was with the negro ?" demanded Wacora.

" His master," repeated Maracota.

" Warren Rody ?"

Maracota nodded.

" I heard their talk," he said.

" What did they say ?" asked the young chief.

" At first, I could not hear---they spoke in whispers.  After a time they grew angry.  Warren abused Crookleg and struck him.  The black man uttered a fierce oath and leaped over the wall of the fort at the side opposite to where I lay hid."

" Did you hear their conversation before they quarrelled ?"

" I heard the pale-face say Crookleg had only half done his errand and must return to complete it.  The black refused.  It was then the other got angry and struck him."

" This is very strange, Maracota.  It is some treachery I cannot understand.  The negro must be found and questioned."

" Well, Massa Injun, dat ain't hard to do.  He, he, he !"

Had the fiend of darkness himself risen between the two Indians, they could not have been more startled than when these words were uttered in their ears, for it was Crookleg who spoke.

The darkey appeared delighted at the effect his sudden appearance had created, and continued for some time to chuckle in great glee.

" Yas ! here be de 'dentical nigga wot you was a wishin' for.  You hab found him 'ithout gwin far. He, he, he !"

Wacora turned sternly towards him.

" And having found you, wretch, I mean to keep you till I've made you speak the truth."

" De trufe, Massa Injun, am what dis ole nigga always 'peak.  He can't help it, kase it comes so nat'ral to him.  Trufe an' innocence is dis chile's on'y riches, t'ank Heaven !"

The look which accompanied this impious speech was almost diabolical.

Wacora cut him short in an attempt to continue his speech, by a command instantly to make known what Warren Rody wanted, with what message he had been charged, and to whom.

Crookleg, however, was not easily taken at a disadvantage.

" Well, Massa Injun, I don't mind tellin' you somet'ing, but I don't like talkin' afore other folk.  You send dis indiwiddle away," pointing to Maracota, " an' ole Crook 'll tell you all about it.  He meant to do so, when he comed here so sudden."

With a sign the chief dismissed Maracota, and telling the black to follow, led him a little distance further from the town.

A long, and apparently interesting conversation ensued, in which Crookleg's gesticulations were, as usual, violent, while the young chief, with arms folded, and brows knit, listened to his narration.

It was late ere they separated, the negro hobbling back in the direction of the ruin, while Wacora returned to his uncle's dwelling.

## CHAPTER XVIII.

### A LOVE MEETING.

THE old fort, as already said, was in a ruinous condition.

It had at one time been a stronghold of the Spaniards, but on their quitting that part of the country, it had been suffered to fall into decay.

Early in the morning succeeding Wacora's interview with Crookleg, two persons stood conversing near the inner wall of the ruin.

They were Sansuta and Warren Rody.

The Indian girl had stolen from her father's house unnoticed by the few early risers, and with cautious steps had gained the fort.

Warren's presence at such a distance from Tampa Bay, as well as Crookleg's attendance upon him, were thus explained.

"I am very grateful to you, Sansuta, for coming here to meet me."

"I am afraid I have done wrong."

"Wrong! What can you mean?"

"That I am deceiving my father, my kind father; but it is for the last time."

"The last time?"

"Yes, I have determined that this shall be our last meeting. I could not endure my father's reproaches, if he knew that I betrayed his confidence."

"Do you doubt my love for you, Sansuta? Will it not make up for Oluski's anger?"

"Warren!"

The reproachful tone in which Sansuta uttered his name, recalled young Rody to himself.

He immediately changed his tactics.

"But why talk of Oluski's anger? Rather speak of my love. Surely you do not doubt it?"

The Indian maiden heaved a sigh.

"Sansuta does not doubt you, but she is unhappy."

"Unhappy! Why?"

"Because an Indian girl would make but a poor wife to a white gentleman."

A strange smile crossed the young man's face. He did not, however, interrupt her.

"If Sansuta cared for you less, she would not have been here this morning; she would not have seen you again."

"Come, come, dearest, you alarm yourself without reason. Need I keep telling you how much I love you—how I have always loved you? Have we not grown up together? What more natural than love like mine?"

"But your father——"

"He will not object. Why should he? Is he not Oluski's best friend?"

"Yes, they are friends, but still——"

Warren saw that the girl was nervous and alarmed. He lost no time in re-assuring her.

"And, after all, dearest, we need not tell them of our love until we are sure of their consent. In the meantime, let us think only of ourselves. You have not yet told me what I longed to hear."

"What is that?"

"The whispered assurance that your heart is mine!"

A painful struggle was evidently taking place in the maiden's breast. Filial duty and self-reproach contended with that feeling, nurtured by the soft blandishments of the scoundrel by her side.

In such a contest love is always the victor.

This case was not exceptional. Softly murmuring the young man's name, Sansuta hid her head upon his shoulder.

His arm enclasped her waist.

The confession had been made. The die was cast!

They were both startled by a sound heard near. It was like some one sighing.

Warren, with the eye of a lynx, searched among the weeds and wild vines, and pierced through the foliage on all sides, but saw nothing.

Reassuring her with honeyed words, he then led the girl away from the spot.

As soon as they had disappeared, a man's form was seen standing upon the place they had last occupied; while another was visible at no great distance from it.

He who first made appearance seemed utterly bowed down with grief, whilst a cloud black as night was visible on his brow.

It was the chief, Wacora!

With an angry and contemptuous action he flung some pieces of money to the other who had followed him, and who was the negro Crookleg.

"Begone! Wacora may use you for his revenge—you shall not witness his grief. Begone!"

The black picked up the coins, grinned hideously, and hobbled away.

Wacora stood for some time rapt in his own sad thoughts. Then, turning his back upon the old fort, he retraced his steps to Oluski's dwelling.

The old chief found but a dull guest in his nephew during that and many succeeding days.

He would sit for hours seemingly lost to all that was passing around him.

Then starting up suddenly, he would stride out of the dwelling with rapid steps, pass out of the town, and on to the adjoining woods, plunging into their depths, to emerge from them hours after, sullen and abstracted as ever!

His anxiety to return to his own tribe seemed to have passed away; and day by day he deferred his departure on the plea of some trivial excuse for remaining.

He watched Sansuta's movements, however, with the jealous care a mother might exercise over her infant child. Every look, word, and action seemed to command his closest scrutiny.

The girl often trembled as she caught the young chief's eye gazing upon her. His stern demeanour agitated her. She suspected that he knew her secret; although neither by word or action did he betray the knowledge.

Oluski was amazed at his conduct. In their conversation there was a renewed bitterness when they talked of the pale-faces, and their actions. It astonished the old Seminole chief. He could not understand the sudden growth of such an unjust antipathy; he therefore became more reticent, and would sit for hours without exchanging a word with his nephew.

Time passed in this manner until the period for the annual migration of the tribe to Tampa Bay. To Oluski's surprise, Wacora signified his intention to accompany them, and along with them he went.

## CHAPTER XIX.

### A CHANGED SCENE.

STILL greater surprise was in store for the Seminole chief and his tribe.

The Indians stood as if petrified, when they came within sight of the well-known hill.

Upon its table-top, and visible for miles around, stood a frame mansion, in all the glitter of fresh paint.

When Oluski first saw it, he uttered an exclamation of agonized anger, at the same time catching hold of Wacora's arm—but for its friendly support, he would have fallen to the ground.

"Look, Wacora; look yonder' What is it we see?"

As he spoke, he passed his hand across his eyes to shade off the blinding sun.

No; they had not deceived him; there was no glamour over them. The sun's beams were shining brightly upon a house.

His nephew looked sadly into the old man's face, fervently pressing his hand. He dared not trust himself to speak.

"And this is the act of a friend. So much for my blind faith in the traitor's deceitful words. May the curse of the Great Spirit fall on him and his!"

Wacora added—"Yes; may both be accursed!"

Then drawing his uncle away from the contemplation of the painful sight, he conducted him to a neighbouring grove of oaks, the tribe halting near the spot.

A council of the chief men was instantly called, and a plan of action resolved on.

Oluski and Wacora were commissioned to visit the white settlement, and demand the reason for this scandalous usurpation.

The Indians proceeded no farther.

That night they encamped upon the spot where they had halted, and early the next morning the two chiefs departed on their mission.

As they approached the hill, another surprise awaited them.

Surrounding it was a strong wooden stockade, with substantially-built block-houses at regular distances from each other. Behind the palisading men were seen, as if watching their approach, and ready to receive them in a hostile manner.

"See!" cried Wacora, "they are prepared for our reception. The robbers have determined to maintain themselves in their stolen possession."

"Yes, yes! I see. But let us not act rashly. We will first make an appeal in the name of justice. If they refuse that, then we must prove ourselves worthy the blood in our veins!—worthy of our ancestors! Oh, I would rather be lying among them in yonder graveyard, than that this should have arisen! The fault has been mine, and upon me let fall the punishment. Come on!"

They reached the central block-house, and were summoned to halt by one of the settlers, who, gun in hand, stood by the entrance.

"Who are you? What do you want?"

Oluski answered—

"White man! go tell your governor that Oluski, the Seminole chief, would speak with him."

The sentinel answered sharply—

"The governor is not here. He is at his house, and cannot be disturbed."

Wacora's hand clutched his tomahawk. Oluski, perceiving the act, laid hold of his nephew's arm.

"Patience, Wacora; patience! The time for bloodshed will come soon enough. For my sake be patient!"

Then turning to the sentry, he continued, his eyes flashing in their sockets—"Fool!" said he, "go with my message; the lives of hundreds may depend upon it. Tell your chief that I am here! Bring him instantly before me!"

The dignity of the old Indian's manner struck the man with respect. Perhaps the nervous twitching of Wacora's fingers about the handle of his tomahawk had also its effect.

Calling out to a comrade who was near, and placing him at the post, he hastened off towards the house.

The two Indians, without exchanging speech, patiently awaited his return.

There was evidently some commotion within the frame dwelling at the reception of the news, as several men, well armed, were observed hurrying off in different directions, and taking station along the line of the stockade.

Shortly after, the man who had been sent was seen coming back.

Throwing open the strong slab door, he beckoned the two chiefs to enter.

They did so, and then, leading them inside the block house, the man told them there to await the governor's arrival. It was not long delayed.

Elias Rody was seen coming forth from his new mansion, followed by five or six stalwart settlers!

All save himself carried rifles.

The Indians stood still as statues.

They made no movement to lessen the distance between themselves and the white men.

At length Elias Rody and Oluski stood face to face.

A close observer might have detected signs of fear in the governor's countenance.

Despite his assumed boldness of bearing, he found it hard to look into the face of the man he had so cruelly wronged.

It was he, however, who first broke the silence so painful to himself.

"What does Oluski wish to say to me?"

"What is the meaning of this?" asked the chief, pointing to the mansion as he spoke.

"That is my new residence."

"By what right have you built it on this ground?"

"By the right of possession—bought and paid for."

Oluski started as if a shot had struck him.

"Bought and paid for? Dog of a liar! What do you mean?"

"Only that I have built my house upon land purchased from you. Your memory appears bad, my old Indian friend."

"Purchased from me? When—how?"

"Do you already forget the guns, powder, and valuables I gave you? Fie, fie! you are trying to cheat me! Surely you must remember your bargain! But if your memory fails you, these gentlemen," here Rody pointed to the settlers, "these gentlemen are prepared to certify to the truth of what I say."

Oluski only groaned.

The audacious treachery of the white man was beyond his simple belief.

Wacora, burning with indignation, spoke for him.

"False wretch, the lie these men are ready to swear to is too monstrous to be believed, even were they upon their oaths! Those gifts were thrust upon my uncle, falsely bestowed as the lands he gave you were falsely claimed for services done to him! Your black heart never conceived a generous thought or a just deed! All was for a treacherous end—the betrayal of this noble-minded chief, as much your superior as the Deity you profess to worship is above the white man himself! Wacora despises you! Wacora has said it!"

He drew Oluski towards him, and stood erect and proud in the consciousness of right before the trembling usurper and his adherents.

The aged chief had recovered himself while his nephew was speaking.

"What Wacora has said is good, and he only utters my own thoughts. I came here ready to receive atonement for the wrong done me and my people. I now see that there is a darker depth of treachery in you even than this which has robbed a confiding man of his best-loved possession. I, Oluski, the Seminole, spit at and despise you! I have spoken!"

With a kingly dignity the old chief folded his blanket around him, and leaning on his nephew's arm, slowly departed from the spot.

Rody and his followers, as if transfixed by the withering contempt with which the Indians had treated them, suffered the two to depart without molestation.

But they now redoubled their watchfulness, stationed additional sentinels around the stockade, and looked after the arms and ammunition, with which they would, no doubt, have to defend the usurped possession.

The small cloud that had been slowly gathering over the settlement was growing dark and portentous. The soft breeze was rapidly rising to a storm.

The people of the settlement, alarmed by the news of the interview between Rody and the Indian chiefs, which spread rapidly among them, hastened to take measures for the safety of their families. The women and children were hurriedly brought in from the outlying plantations, and lodged in temporary abodes within the stockade, whilst provisions in plenty were carried to the same place.

The war signal had sounded, and before long the work of carnage would commence.

## CHAPTER XX.

### STILL ANOTHER SORROW.

ISAPPOINTED and chafed, the two chiefs returned in all haste to the Indian encampment.

But few words had been spoken between them on their way from the hill. A firm pressure of his uncle's hand was proof that Wacora, once embarked in the impending contest, would remain faithful to its end.

It needs no speech among true men to establish confidence. Between the two chiefs it was mutual.

As they neared the spot where the tribe had pitched their tents, an unusual excitement was observable. Men and women were conversing in little groups, animated apparently by the receipt of some startling news.

The two chiefs at first imagined that the result of their interview was already known; but on reflection, the impossibility of the thing became apparent to them, and their surprise was extreme.

All at once they saw Nelatu hastening towards them.

The young man seemed ready to drop, as if from fatigue. His looks told that he was a prey to the keenest anxiety.

On arriving before the two chiefs, he was for some moments unable to speak.

Words rose to his tongue, but they found no articulate utterance. His lips seemed glued together. Drops of sweat glistened on his brow.

The father, with a dreadful prescience of new sorrows, trembled at sight of his son.

"Nelatu," he said, "what anguish awaits me? Of what fresh disaster do you bring the tidings? Speak! speak!"

The young Indian again essayed, but only succeeded in muttering, "Sansuta!"

"FORCED INTO SERVICE."

" Sansuta! What of her? Is she dead? Answer me?

" No; she is not dead. Oh! father, be calm—have courage—she is——"

" Speak, boy, or I shall go mad! What of her?"

" She is gone!"

" Gone! Whither?"

" I have sought her everywhere. I only heard of her departure after you left the encampment. Bury your tomahawk in my brain if you will, for I have been the cause."

" What does the boy rave about? What does it all mean? Has the Great Spirit cursed me in all my hopes? Speak, Nelatu. Where is your sister? You say she is gone. Gone! Gone! With whom?"

" With Warren Rody!"

Oluski uttered a shriek of mingled rage and grief, pressed his hand upon his heart, and reeling, would have fallen to the earth but for Wacora's arm, at that instant thrown around him.

The two young men bent over his prostrate form, which his nephew had gently laid upon the sward.

A few faint, murmuring words escaped from his lips; so faint, indeed, that they were not comprehended by either son or nephew.

The frown which had gathered on his brow in his interview with Elias Rody gradually gave place to a gentle smile. His eyes, for an instant, rested sorrowfully on the face of Nelatu, then on Wacora, and were closed for ever.

With that look had his life ended. The spirit of the Seminole chief had departed to a better land.

Wounded in his friendship, doubly wounded in his pride, cruelly stabbed by the desertion of his own daughter and the weakness of his own son, outraged as friend and father, the old man's heart had burst within his bosom.

Tenderly covering the body with his blanket, Wacora stooped and kissed the cold brow in silence, registering a vow of vengeance upon his murderers.

Nelatu, stunned by the suddenness of the event, hid his face in his hands, and gave way to lamentation and tears.

That evening the remains of their chief were interred in a temporary grave, around which the warriors of the tribe, by their own consent now commanded by Wacora, joined in an oath of sure and ample vengeance. Coupled with their oath was the declaration that war and rapine should not cease until the hill was again their own, and the body of their beloved chief laid peacefully beside the bones of his ancestors.

That night the red pole was erected in their encampment, and under the glare of pine torches was performed around it the fearful scalp-dance of the tribe.

The white sentinels upon the hill saw afar off the fiend-like performance, and, as around echoed in their ears their wi shriek, they turned trembling from the hill, and cursed Elias Rody!

# CHAPTER XXI.

### WACORA CHOSEN CHIEF.

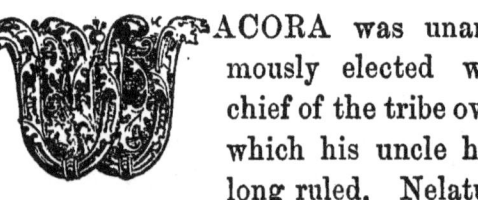ACORA was unanimously elected war chief of the tribe over which his uncle had long ruled. Nelatu's claims were so slight, his ability so deficient, that not one of the warriors wished to nominate him for the important position.

To Wacora the honour was of inestimable value. By its means there was now a hope for the realisation of his long-cherished dream—the redemption of the red-man by the union of all the tribes into one powerful nation.

He instantly dispatched messengers to the braves of his own sub-tribe, summoning them to Tampa Bay, to take part in the conflict.

He was answered by the speedy arrival of a large and well-armed force, who, mingling with Oluski's people, now became one community.

Obedient to his mandate, they continued to preserve an ominously peaceful attitude towards the settlers, who, but for a knowledge to the contrary, might have comforted themselves with a belief that the red-men had left the bay.

But although unseen, their presence was not unfelt. The news of Oluski's death had spread a feeling of alarm among the white colonists, which the heartless and assumed indifference of Elias Rody and his adherents could not dismiss from their minds.

The "governor" seemed to have returned to the courses of his early life. He had for many years been a man of sober habits; but since the building of his new house a change had come over him. He had begun to drink freely, and in the excitement of preparation for the defence of his usurped property, he found a thousand excuses for the indulgence of that appetite so long kept under control.

Still another matter gave discomfort to the governor. His son had been for some time missing from the settlement, and in a mysterious manner. His disappearance had a marked effect on his father's temper, and when not cursing himself for the general discomfort he had caused, he cursed the son for adding to it.

It will thus be seen that although Elias Rody had prepared his own bed, and was obliged to lie upon it, it was proving anything but a bed of roses.

Had it not been for the presence of his daughter Alice, the new mansion in which he now lived, and for which he might yet have to pay dearly, would have been a perfect Pandemonium to him.

That amiable girl, by her gentle behaviour, did much to soften the rude, inharmonious elements around her; and the roughest of her father's roystering companions were silent and respectful in her presence.

She was like a ministering angel among those who had taken refuge within the stockade. She never seemed to tire of attending upon them or their wants. Her kind, sympathetic voice and assiduous care were of inestimable service to the sick.

Nothing, in the meantime, had been heard of her brother Warren.

Crookleg had also disappeared, although no one particularly missed him.

Cris Carrol, the hunter, had not returned to the settlement. In some distant savanna he was no doubt tranquilly passing his time, at peace with all the world. Such was the condition of affairs.

The first preparations for strife between the whites and Indians had been made; and to several other outrages, similar to that committed by Elias Rody, may be traced the causes of that Seminole war which cost the Government of the United States some thousands of lives, along with several millions of dollars, to say nought of the reputation of six hitherto distinguished generals.

## CHAPTER XXII.

### A CONVERSATION BETWEEN COUSINS.

THE tranquil state of affairs did not last for long.

The Indians, eager to revenge Oluski's death, were impatient of the restraint Wacora would have imposed upon them, and, at a council convened for that purpose, they determined to attack the stockade upon the hill.

This determination was hastened by several *rencontres* which had taken place in the outlying districts.

A small party of the red-men, led by Maracota, had pillaged and destroyed a plantation.

Near the bay they had been met by some of the white settlers as they were returning from their work of destruction.

In the *mêlée* which ensued a number of Indians were killed, whilst their white adversaries met with little loss.

These and some individual cases of contest had worked the red-men up to a pitch of savage earnestness that took all Wacora's temporising power to restrain.

He knew the character of the people he had to deal with too well to hazard opposition to their will, the more so as his own desire for vengeance was as deep and earnest, but more deadly than theirs.

One thought occupied his mind nobler than that of revenge—the regeneration of the Indian race.

A chimera it may have been, but still his great ambition.

He thus spoke to the assembled chiefs—

"I do not urge upon you to withhold vengeance for injuries done to our race by the white enemy. I can only desire to make it more full and terrible. This is but the beginning of a long list of retributions, the overflowing of accumulated wrongs, the first step towards freedom and redemption! To take that step we must be patient until certain of success. Then begins a warfare that will only end with the annihilation of our hated enemies and in a new existence for the red-man! Have I spoken well?"

Loud approbation greeted him from the assembled warriors; but such is the inconsistency of human character that individually they devised means for immediate retaliation on the settlers.

Hence the several encounters which had already taken place.

Nelatu, mortified at his own weakness, was among the warriors addressed by Wacora.

On returning from the council, the young chief approached his cousin.

"Nelatu, you would do something to make up for your blind infatuation, that has led to such misfortunes?"

"I would, Wacora, I would. My father's face seems always before me, reproaching me as my sister's destroyer."

"Then action is the only way by which to shake off the remorseful feeling. Our efforts have till now been fruitless in tracing the spot to which your sister has been carried. She must be found, and the punishment of the guilty made sure."

"Not Sansuta. You would not injure her?"

Wacora smiled sadly, as he pressed his hand upon his heart.

"No, Nelatu, I would not injure your sister. Alas! I had already learned to love her. I would not hurt her for worlds. It is the wretch who has carried her away. I would have him suffer a thousand deaths, and every death more terrible than the other!"

"Tell me, what can I do? If I remain idle, I shall die!"

"Take three or four of my own people, follow every trail that promises to lead to where they are concealed, and having found the monster, bring him to me alive."

Wacora's eyes, as he uttered these words, blazed with passion.

"I would rather go alone," said Nelatu.

"As you please; but remember, that there is one man you dare not trust, and yet he may be the means of finding Sansuta."

"His name?"

"Crookleg, the negro."

"But he, too, is missing."

"I know it, and therefore he can lead you to their hiding-place, if he can be found. With Crookleg to assist you, you may succeed; without him your search will be fruitless."

"How am I to find him?"

"By diligent search. He is not near

the spot, but yet not so distant as to be ignorant of what is passing. He has the cunning of the wild cat; remember that."

"I'll be a match for him, never fear, cousin."

Wacora glanced pityingly at the simple youth.

He thought of his confiding nature, and felt that if the only chance of finding Sansuta lay in cunning, she would never be discovered.

"Well, Nelatu, I have given you the best advice I can. Will you undertake the search?"

"I will!"

"When?"

"At once, Wacora."

With these words the cousins separated.

## CHAPTER XXIII.

### THE STRAYED CANOE.

HAT night Nelatu left the Indian camp.

Wacora had given him a few hints by which he thought his search for Crookleg might be facilitated.

He had suggested that the old negro lay concealed within the neighbouring swamp.

This wilderness, difficult to traverse, was of great extent.

It was only by a knowledge of its intricate paths that it could be successfully explored.

Nelatu, fully appreciating the difficulty of his undertaking, was more than usually depressed.

The journey through the track of dry timber was easy enough.

On emerging from it he found himself on a broad savanna, on the other side of which lay the swamp to which Wacora had directed him.

Its gloomy appearance struck a chill to the young chief's heart.

Could it by any possibility be the place selected by Warren for Sansuta's concealment?

He almost hoped his search for her in its sombre fastnesses might prove futile.

Its aspect was especially forbidding at the time Nelatu reached it, which was in the early morning.

A heavy fog rose from its dark waters, clinging around the rank vegetation, and veiling the mosses and spectral limbs of the decayed trees.

A fetid breath exhaled from the thick undergrowth, and the air seemed charged with poison.

No note of bird was heard, no bloom of flower seen.

Death in life was everywhere apparent.

Carefully, and with the quick natural

instinct of his race, Sansuta's brother struck upon a well-defined trail, leading inwardly from the borders of the morass.

Following this with care, he had soon made considerable progress.

The sun rising higher as he advanced, only revealed more clearly the gloomy character of the scene.

The thick mist became dispelled, the verdure, dark but rich, glistened with drops of moisture, and the ghostly moss waved to and fro, stirred by a gentle breeze that had helped to dissipate the fog.

With the bright sky, however, there came a corresponding lightness over the young man's spirit, and a doubt arose in his mind as to the guilt of his former friend.

"I cannot believe all that he has been accused of. Perhaps he is not guilty of carrying off Sansuta.

"I always trusted him. Why should he be so evil, without a suspicion having crossed my mind that he was so?

"He has not been seen since she disappeared, but yet Crookleg may be the guilty one.

"If all I have been told be true, and Warren be the man, he shall bitterly pay for his crime. But I will not believe it until I am convinced 'tis so."

It will be seen that Nelatu was still a firm friend, ready to doubt even villany.

Suddenly the trail he was following came to an end.

A deep black lagoon was before his feet.

How to cross it?

Its unrippled bosom showed it to be deep.

Here and there jagged cypress stumps, to which clung drooping parasites, stood out of it.

Nelatu felt that the trail he had followed was purposely terminated at the edge of the lake, doubtless to be discovered on its opposite shore.

How to cross it?

That was the question.

Stooping, he scanned the shore, but failed to trace any further evidence of the footsteps of man.

He was on the point of retracing his path, in order to look for a trail, when he was arrested by a faint sound, as from a movement in the water.

It was very faint, but unmistakable in its character.

It was the stroke of an oar!

He strained his eyes to catch a view of the boat, which he felt sure was traversing the lake.

After some time spent in the endeavour, his scrutiny was rewarded.

A strange tableau was revealed to him.

At a distance appeared the shadowy form of a canoe, in which two figures were seated.

The fog, like a dull silver veil, was still spread over the lagoon, and his efforts to recognize the phantom-like forms were unavailing.

The intervening curtain of vapour baffled even the keen eyesight of an Indian.

He hallooed to the spectral figures, until the swamp re-echoed his shouts.

In vain.

No response came from the silent voyagers.

He fancied that the measured pulling of the oars for an instant ceased, but so dim and unreal did it all appear, that he began to doubt the evidence of his senses.

As he gazed the canoe glided silently out of sight.

Muttering an angry adjuration at the ghostly oarsmen, he threw himself upon the ground.

Overcome with the fatiguing journey, and dispirited by his fruitless search, he soon fell into a deep slumber.

The last film of the fog was now dispelled by the powerful rays of the sun.

Birds sang in the trees above him, and from the black waters of the lagoon a huge caiman crawled up the banks to bask in the noontide glare.

Still Nelatu slumbered.

He slept until the meridian heat had passed, and the evening approached, seeming to lull all nature into silence.

The young man's sleep was placid. With his head pillowed on his arm, he lay like one dead.

From this sweet unconsciousness, he awoke with a start.

A rippling sound as of some craft cleaving the water once more fell upon his ear.

Had the phantom canoe returned?

A glance answered the question.

Drifting near the shore was an empty dug-out.

The broken manilla rope, dragging at the stern, told him why it was adrift.

Without hesitation he plunged into the water, and in a few strokes reached the straying craft.

Scrambling into it, he seized an oar found lying in its bottom, and paddled back to the place whence he had started. Placing his gun ready beside him, he again paddled off, and rowed into the centre of the lake, steering his course, as nearly as he could remember, in the direction which, in the morning, he had observed the canoe to take.

The spot, as he had marked it, was near a huge cypress tree.

It proved to be at a greater distance than he thought, and the sun had well sunk in the western sky before he arrived at it.

Once there he came to a stop. Those he sought had evidently either gone further out into the open water of the lagoon or had made for one or other of the numerous narrow canals which debouched into it.

Selecting that which appeared of the greatest width, he plied his oar and advanced towards it.

# CHAPTER XXIV.

### A SMOKE INTERRUPTED.

LTHOUGH Cris Carrol was absent from the immediate neighbourhood of the settlement, he was none the less informed of what had happened since his departure.

Several of the colonists, alarmed at the prospect of affairs, had quickly left Tampa Bay, and, meeting with the hunter, had told him of the events that had transpired within the past month.

The backwoodsman's foresight had not deceived him.

The whites, by which he meant Elias and his followers, had not heeded his advice, and worse had come of it.

The hunter was nothing, if not oracular.

"Wal," said he, "Governor Rody thought himself smart when he set to work buildin' that thar frame-house of his'n on the red-man's ground, but I reckon he'll pay for it yet in bloody scalps and broken bones. Confound the old cormorant; his house will cause all them poor white settlers no end of trouble. It don't bear thinkin' on, that it don't. As for his black-hearted whelp of a son, darn me if I wouldn't like to put an ounce o' lead into his carcase, if it war only to larn him some human feelin'."

"But won't you go back to the settlement now, and see if your presence can do any good?"

To this question, propounded by one of the fugitive settlers, Cris answered—

"Good! What good can I do now? No, lad, the fat's in the fire this time, and, maybe, I may better help some poor critter away from the place than anigh it. I'll tell ye what it is, and it ain't no use denyin' it. Them there red devils means mischief, and the old cuss Rody knows it by this time. The chief, Oluski, what you tell me air dead, war worth a whole settlement of Rodys—barrin' one—that is, barrin' one."

"And who may that be?"

"Who but his darter. The most beautiful gal that this coon ever set eyes on. Bless her, I hope no hurt won't come to her, and there shan't either, if Cris Carrol can prevent it."

In this manner did the honest hunter comment on the alarming news brought by the fugitives from Tampa Bay.

Not that he approached the spot too closely. No; he had formed an idea of the manner in which he might be most useful; and, to do so, he must carefully avoid any appearance of interference between the contending parties.

He, therefore, pursued his occupation

of hunting; but contrived materially to narrow the circle of his excursions.

Often as the image of Alice Rody presented itself to his mind, he would heave a painful sigh.

"How such a gal came to be a child of that old trait'rous heathen is more nor I can reckon up. It's one of them thar things as philosophers call start-lers!"

In one of these moralising, wandering moods the old hunter was seated on a tree stump on the afternoon of a day that had been more than usually fatigu-ing to him.

He knocked the ashes from his pipe, took a plug of tobacco from his pouch, and began to cut up a supply for another smoke.

"Ah!" muttered he, shaking his head, "I remember the time when there was happiness in the savannas, and when them red-skins were ready to help the white man rather than fight agin them. Them times is gone from hyar for ever!"

He struck a light with his flint, and applied it to his pipe.

Just as he had puffed two or three small clouds of smoke, and was preparing to enjoy himself to the fullest extent, a flash suddenly appeared, the pipe was knocked from his mouth, and the whizz of a bullet sounded unpleasantly close to his ears!

To grasp his rifle and shelter himself behind a tree, on the opposite side to that from which the shot proceeded, was for the hunter but the work of an instant.

"Red-skins, by the eternal! I know it by the twang of that rough-cast bullet."

Whether red-skins or white men he did not find it easy to be certain, although he was up to every move in such an emergency.

He knew that to look in the direction of the shot was to expose himself to almost certain death.

He listened with breathless anxiety for the slightest sound, which might give evidence of the movements of the enemy.

But everything remained perfectly still.

Adopting a very old *ruse*, he stuck his skin-cap upon the barrel of his rifle, and held it out a few inches beyond the trunk of the tree, by the side of which he had ensconced himself.

A flash, a report, and it was pierced by a bullet!

He was now fully satisfied that there was but one enemy with whom he had to cope.

Had there been more, the first bullet, which struck the pipe from his mouth, would have been followed by another as quickly, but probably more surely aimed.

With a rapid glance he surveyed the ground behind him.

It was covered with undergrowth and fallen timber.

Cris Carrol's resolution was at once taken.

He fell flat upon the earth, and noiselessly gliding away, reached a tree, distant some paces, and in an oblique direction from the one he had moved awayfro m.

From that spot he made his way to

another, at a greater angle, and about equally distant from the second.

The movements were affected with such agile stealthiness, as to be entirely unperceived by his still unseen enemy.

By the change of position he now commanded a side view of his unknown antagonist, who, unsuspicious of it, was keeping a close watch upon Carrol's supposed shelter.

To raise his rifle to his shoulder was a natural action of the old hunter.

Instead of pulling the trigger, however, some idea seemed to cross his mind, and pausing, he scanned his adversary.

He saw it was Maracota who had fired at him !

Carrol knew Maracota as a faithful and devoted follower of the late chief, and he felt loth to take his life, although he might easily have done so.

The better thought prevailed.

He felt convinced that the bullet fired by the Indian had been aimed in reality at one for whom Maracota had mistaken him.

Advancing cautiously towards the unconscious warrior, the old backwoodsman crept from tree to tree until he was close upon him.

Not anticipating an attack from the rear, and still fancying he commanded the hiding-place of the white man, Maracota, in spite of his Indian cunning, was completely in the white man's power.

A loud shout, a quick bound, and Cris Carrol had the Indian in his grasp.

With one hand upon his throat, the hunter had pinned him to the earth.

" Not a word, you darned catamount, or I'll run my knife into your ribs ! So you thought to circumvent me, did yer, with your Injun treachery ? What would you say now if I war to raise your ha'r, 'stead of letting you take mine ?"

Maracota could make no reply to the question, as the pressure on his throat completely stopped his breath as well as speech.

The backwoodsman saw by the expression upon the Indian's face, that his own surmise had been correct.

He was not the victim Maracota would have doomed to death.

It was a mistake, but rather a serious one.

Loosening his hold, he suffered the astonished Maracota to rise to his feet.

" Yes ; I can tell you've made a random shot at me. Next time, try and see a man's face 'fore you pulls trigger on him, or it might be awk'ard. There's no harm done, only a worse shot nor yours I never saw. I'd eat my rifle, stock, lock, and barrel, afore I'd own to sich shooting. Who war it ye war arter ?"

Having at length recovered breath, the Indian was able to answer.

" I took you for the White Chief's son, Warren Rody."

" Much obleeged for the compliment. Do I look such a skunk as that fellow? If I do, put a brace of bullets into me, and we won't quarrel."

The warrior grimly smiled.

" Maracota has sworn to avenge Oluski's death. Warren Rody must die !"

"A BULLET HAD PIERCED HIS BRAIN."

"Wal, let him die. I shan't stop you from riddin' the world of such as he. What made you follow my trail?"

"It was no trail I followed. I have been seeking one from the north; yours came from the east."

"Right you air; that's whar I hail from last."

"Have you seen anything of him, or of Sansuta?"

"Hark hyar, Injun. Altho' I might draw blood in the scoundrel if I saw him, I ain't a *man-hunter*, and that's why I ain't been a follerin' any trail of his'n."

Maracota's eager look gave place to one of despondency, as he muttered—

"Not found yet! Where can they be?"

"Ah! whar? It ain't Warren as has hid whar he can't be found. Some knowin' hand has put him up to it."

"Yes, Maracota think so. It must be the negro, Crookleg."

"Crookleg! Is that all-fired nigger varmint mixed up with him? That makes a brace of the durndest hounds as ever run together. Who told you Crookleg helped young Rody?"

"The chief thinks so."

"Wal, then, I'll bet a 'possum skin agin a musk rat's that he's right. Your chief, Wacora, is as likely an Injun at reck'nin' up the merits o' a case as this coon knows on. Now you've missed liftin' my scalp, what do you intend doin'?"

"Go on looking for the chief who stole Oluski's heart, find him, and kill him."

The glance that accompanied these words was full of deadly determination.

"Wal, go, and good luck attend ye. Don't ask me to jine ye. I tell you I ain't no man-hunter nor never will be; only if either of them thar scamps should be out walkin' whar I chance to be, they had better have met with a mad b'ar, than this hyar Cris Carrol. Never mind sayin' a word about that bad shot o' yourn. The moment I seed you I knowed you didn't mean it for me, only next time be more partiklar, that's all."

Without making reply, Maracota turned away, and was soon lost under the shadows of the forest.

As soon as he was out of sight, the old hunter renewed his preparations for a smoke.

Drawing from his pouch (which seemed to contain everything that the heart of a hunter could desire) another pipe, he was soon once more sending clouds of blue smoke up into the air.

"If that Maracota meets Warren Rody or Crookleg, he'll be an awkward customer to either or both on 'em; and that he may meet 'em he has Cris Carrol's best prayers and wishes."

With this homely but sincere expression of his desires, the backwoodsman ceased to think of the deadly danger lately threatening himself.

## CHAPTER XXV.

### PREPARING FOR THE ATTACK.

 H E Indians had, at length, determined upon making an attack upon Elias Rody's stronghold.

The governor had got wind of their intention through a spy, a slave belonging to the tribe, who had turned informer through his seductive offers.

A meeting of the settlers within the stockade was at once called.

"Fellow citizens," said Rody, addressing them, "I have received some information that our enemies have resolved upon attacking us. It is my duty to tell you this in order that every man may be prepared to defend himself and his family. One thing I would have you remember; this war will be one of extermination; therefore, be careful not to waste a bullet. Let every pull upon your trigger send an Indian to his long account. Let the cry be 'no quarter!'"

"Perhaps that'll be their motto too," remarked a voice in the crowd.

"I perceive, sir," replied Rody, a little nettled at the running commentary on his speech, "I perceive that there are still one or two dissatisfied people amongst us. Let them step forward, and declare themselves. We want neither renegades or traitors in our midst."

"That's so!" the voice replied.

"Again I say let those displeased with my views step boldly out, and allow me to answer any objections they may raise. I've done nothing I am ashamed of. I blush for nothing that I do."

"No, you're past blushing!" was the ironical rejoinder.

Suppressed titters ran round the assemblage at these pertinent remarks of the unknown, and the governor's temper was not improved by observing the effect the words had produced on his hearers.

"I scorn to answer the fellow who is afraid to show himself, but I warn you all to be prepared for a desperate contest. We have only ourselves to look to for our defence. We are in the hands of Providence."

"We are!"

This sudden change from jeering comment to deep solemnity of utterance on the part of the unknown speaker, struck awe into the crowd, and caused Rody to turn pale.

In the hands of Providence!

Yes, for good or evil. For punishment or reward.

The thought expressed in this manner was too much for the governor.

He dismissed the meeting with a hurried admonition to be prepared for the worst.

As he re-entered his house, he encountered his daughter face to face.

"Father, I was about to seek you," said she. "They tell me that you have heard bad news?"

"Bad enough, girl! The redskins are going to attack us."

"Is there no hope?"

"Hope, for what?"

"That this bloodshed may be avoided. Will they not listen to an offer of reconciliation?"

"And who would dare to make it?"

"Dare, father! I do not understand you. It is the duty of those who have done wrong to contrive by concession to atone for it, and, if possible, make peace."

"But who has done wrong?"

Alice did not answer in words, but the look she bestowed upon her father was eloquence itself.

"I see what you're thinking about, my girl. It's hard that inside of my own home I should meet with reproaches. Isn't it enough for me to have to bear the sneers and taunts of others, without being forced to listen to them from you?"

"Father!"

"Oh, yes; now you'll try to say you didn't mean to reproach me, but it won't do. I see it in your face, and, there, your eyes are full of tears; that's the way with you girls, when you can't use your tongues, you have always a stock of tears ready. But blubbering won't mend this matter; it's got to be settled with blows."

"Oh! father, can nothing be done?"

"Nothing, but prepare for the worst. Now, girl, stop your crying, or you'll drive me stark mad. I'll tell you what it is, I'm just in that sort of state, that if I don't do something, I shall go clean out of my mind. What with the worrying work here, and the grumbling discontent of a few paltry hounds about the settlement, I don't know how I keep my senses about me!"

The angry mood into which he had worked himself, was, however, no novelty to his daughter. She had of late seen it too often, and sorrowfully noted the change.

Still, she was a brave girl, and knowing she had a duty to perform, she did it fearlessly.

"Oh, father," she exclaimed, apologizingly, "I did not mean to reproach you. If my looks betrayed my thoughts, I cannot help them, much as I may regret giving you pain. What I wanted to say was, that if there is any honourable way to avoid this bloodshed, it should be tried. There is no disgrace in acknowledging a fault."

"Who has committed one?"

"You know wrongs have been done by white people against the Indians, not alone now, but ever since the two races have been brought together. We are no better than others; but we can avoid their errors by trying to remedy the grievances they complain of."

Old Rody stamped the floor with rage; his daughter's remarks made him wince. Conscience, which he deemed asleep, was at work, and upon the tongue of his own child had found utterance.

"Begone, girl!" he cried, "before I

forget that you are my own flesh and blood. You insult me beyond endurance. I will manage affairs my own way, without impediment from you. Aye, not only my own affairs, but the affairs of all here. I will have blind obedience; I demand it, and will exact it. Begone!"

His daughter looked him boldly in the face.

"Be it so, father," she answered; "I have done my duty—will always do it. Think, however, before it is too late, that to your conduct in this matter, the groans of widows and the sighs of orphans may be laid. The happiness or misery of many rests upon your single word. It is an awful risk—reflect upon it, dear father, reflect!"

Her proud bearing gave place to tears. Her womanly heart was full to overflowing. It conquered her spirit for a time; and as she parted from her father's presence, she felt that the last hope of peace had vanished.

"By the eternal powers!" cried he, "this will prove too much for me. It must come to an end!"

As Rody uttered these words, he drew from his pocket a flask and applied it to his lips.

It was a bottle of brandy. It seemed the last friend left him.

## CHAPTER XXVI.

### FORCED INTO SERVICE.

FTER entering the narrow stretch of water, Nelatu, for some time, plied his paddle with vigour.

He then paused to examine the place. Sedges and cane-brakes grew thickly down to the water's edge. There appeared no passage through them.

Resuming his course, he attentively watched for any sign of habitation, but for a long time without success.

Just as he was turning the head of the canoe again in the direction of the lagoon, an object, floating on the surface, attracted his attention.

It was an oar. A glance convinced him that it was the fellow of the one he held in his hand.

Reanimated by this assuring proof that he was going in the right direction, he fished it up, and abandoning the more laborious mode of paddling, he adjusted the oars in the rowlocks, and bending to them, made more rapid way.

He kept his eyes turning to right and left, on the look-out for a landing-place, which he now felt assured could not be far distant.

His scrutiny was at length rewarded.

A few hundred yards from where he had picked up the floating oar, a post was seen sticking up out of the bank.

To this was attached a Manilla rope, the broken strands of which showed it to be the other portion of that fastened to the stern of the canoe.

The clue was found.

Those he had dimly seen in the morning, were doubtless close at hand.

He ran the craft in shore, fastened it securely to the post, and landed.

With cautious steps he followed the footprints now seen in the soft mud of the bank.

They led to a sheltered spot, upon which a rude hut had been erected.

The sound of a man's voice arrested his steps.

"He, he! I 'clare it makes this chile larf, to t'ink about de trubble dat's brewin' for them. De long time am comin' round at last. I'se bin a waitin' for it, but it am comin' now."

It was Crookleg who spoke; but for the time, he said no more.

A stunning blow from Nelatu's clubbed rifle—which would have crushed any skull but that of a negro—felled him senseless to the ground.

On recovering consciousness, he found himself bound in a most artistic manner by a thong of deer-skin, which Nelatu had found near the hut.

"Hush!" said the Indian, in a half-whisper; "not a word, except to answer my questions. Don't move, dog, or I'll dash out your brains!"

The negro trembled in every limb.

"Is young Warren Rody inside that hut?"

Crookleg shook his head.

"Where is he?"

"Don't know, Massa Injun; don't know nuffin 'bout him."

"Liar!"

"By him bressed life, massa, dis chile don't know."

"Answer me — where is Warren Rody? I give you one chance for your wretched life. Tell me, where is Warren Rody?"

The raising of a tomahawk above the negro's head convinced him that death would be the sure reward of untruth.

"Don't, massa, don't kill the ole nigger. He'll tell you all he knows. Oh! don't kill me!"

"Speak!"

"He *war* here, but he am gone!"

"Where?"

"Out ob the swamp into the woods."

"And Sansuta?"

"De gal am gone along wid him."

Nelatu groaned.

Warren, then, was guilty.

"Do you know me?" he asked.

"Oh, yes, massa, I knows you well— you am Sansuta's brodder. I tole Warren he war a doin' wrong, but he am so headstrong he would take your sister. Dis chile's begged him not to do it."

"False dog! you are deceiving me."

"I swear, massa 'Latu, I'se speakin' the bressed trufe."

Not deigning to reply, the Indian strode on to the hut, and entered it. It was deserted.

A bead bracelet lying inside attested to the truth of that portion of Crookleg's story which told him that Sansuta had been there.

He returned to the negro.

"Rise!" he said, in a commanding tone.

"I can't, massa; you has tied me so tight I can't move."

"Rise, I tell you," repeated the Indian, with a threatening gesture.

Beginning to obey, the negro rolled over the ground in the direction of the rifle which Nelatu had laid aside in order to tie him.

Could he but reach that, he might defy his captor.

But the Indian was too quick for him.

With a kick which made Crookleg howl with pain, he forced him aside, and secured the weapon himself.

Seeing that his only chance was submission, the negro got upon his feet with some difficulty, and stood awaiting further orders.

Nelatu now unfastened the thongs that bound him.

"Go before me," he said.

Crookleg hobbled forward with a demoniac look upon his face.

They reached the water's edge.

"Is that your canoe?"

"Yes, massa; that dug-out b'long to me."

"Get in."

The black scrambled into the stern.

"Not there—the other end."

Crookleg obeyed.

Nelatu took the vacated seat.

"Now, lay hold of these oars, bend your back, and row me to the place where you landed Warren Rody and my sister. Remember, that if you make the slightest attempt to deceive me, I will bury my tomahawk deep in your brain."

Thus admonished, the negro plied the oars, and the canoe darted rapidly through the water.

## CHAPTER XXVII.

### THE LOST SISTER.

OR more than an hour Crookleg was compelled to use the oars, until they had reached the other side of the lagoon.

Nelatu, silent and wrapped in his own gloomy thoughts, watched his every motion.

It was twilight when they made a landing within a sheltered bay upon that side of the swamp nearest the settlement.

Beyond this lay the woods of which the negro had spoken.

Compelling the black to precede him, Nelatu urged him forward until they had reached a mound covered with bushes.

"Hush! Massa Injun, we am near de place."

"I see no sign of habitation."

"We is near it, for all dat. It ain't a easy ting to find a place like dis 'ere whar dere are nuffin to show but de ground and dese 'ere bushes."

"Quick! lead me to the place!"

"By-am-by, massa, for a mercy's sake hab jist a little patience. 'Twon't do no good to be in a hurry, 'twon't indeed."

Suspecting treachery, Nelatu would hear of no delay.

"Remember, slave! what I threatened you with. Conduct me at once to their hiding place."

"Well, den, Massa Injun, if you must go, step light, or we'll gib Massa Warren de alarm. He's as quick-eared as a rabbit; dat he am. And he may shoot us both afore we know; dat is, if he 'spects you am coming after de gal."

With this caution, to which his companion silently agreed, they skirted the mound to its extreme end, where it seemed to terminate abruptly in a deep chasm.

Once there, Crookleg threw himself upon the ground, motioning the Indian to do the same.

Nelatu complied, still watching for any movement of betrayal on the part of his guide.

With a stealthy hand the negro parted the bushes, and signed to the young man to look through the opening.

He did so.

Before his eyes was the entrance of a cave or grotto.

Inside the entrance a pine-torch, stuck in the ground, illumined a portion of the interior.

The light was obscured by the bushes, and it was only when these were parted that it became visible.

Inside the grotto was Sansuta.

She was reposing upon a bed of moss.

Behind her, on a large boulder of rock, sat Warren Rody!

Nelatu was on the point of rushing forward, when he was stayed by the negro's hand clutching his arm.

"Not yet, massa," he whispered, "you'd be shot afore you'd got two steps in dar, and dis poor ole nigga would nebba get away 'gain. Let me go speak first, and gib Mass' Rody de signal; and den I'll find a way to bring him out to you. Don't you see that'll be de best plan to fix him?"

"I cannot trust you from my sight. Take your hand off my arm! let me go!"

"Oh, massa, I shall be ruined, and murdered complete. Don't you see dat afore you reach him he'd see you and fire? De ole nigga's plan am de best. Let me bring de fox out ob his hole!"

Crookleg spoke reasonably.

Nelatu might, it is true, have easily killed Warren from where he lay, but his sister's presence, Wacora's command, and a certain reluctance to shed blood, stayed his hand.

"Well, then, do it, but on conditions."

"What conditions, Massa Injun? Name 'em, and I'se obey."

"That you bring him away from my sister's side out here into the open ground; that every word you speak shall be loud enough for me to hear. Go!"

"I'll go, massa."

"See!"

As Nelatu uttered this monosyllable, he tapped his rifle.

Crookleg took the hint.

"I'se swear, massa, I do dis ting right! Dis ole nigga don't want no bullet through him karkiss. I'se swear to do as you say!"

With this asseveration he rose erect and entered boldly among the bushes, while Nelatu concealed himself behind them.

Warren started to his feet, calling out—

"Who's there?"

"Hush, Massa Warren! It's only me—ole Crookleg."

"Come in, Crookleg."

"No, Massa Warren, you come out here. I'se want to speak to you 'thout disturbin' the young gal. I'se want to show you somethin'."

With a hasty glance at the slumbering maiden, Warren Rody emerged from the cave.

At the entrance he was suddenly confronted by Nelatu.

"Nelatu!"

A yell of fiendish laughter from Crookleg answered the exclamation.

"He, he, he, he! ho, ho, ho! Oh, dat am de best ting dis ole nigga eber done! Ah, de time am comin' now! Ho, ho! Massa Warren, who kicked de ole dog of a nigga wot fetch an' carry for de white man to de Injun gal? Ha, ha, ha! I 'clare to mercy it am splendid! Now I'll leave you two friends togedder; but don't quarrel—don't! Only remember, Massa Warren, remember Crookleg to your dyin' day!"

With these words the negro darted off, and was soon lost to sight behind the bushes.

Warren stood grating his teeth in impotent rage.

He saw that he had fallen into a trap laid for him by Crookleg.

Nelatu stirred not an inch.

Again young Rody pronounced his name.

"Nelatu!"

"Yes, Nelatu—the brother of Sansuta! Does not the sight of me turn you into stone? Is your heart so hardened that you do not tremble?"

Warren gave a short, mocking laugh.

"Go away from here," he said; "I owe no account of my actions to any one."

"Yes, you owe an account of them to that Great Spirit who is alike your God and mine!"

"Pah! stand aside, I say."

"My arm will brain you if you move a step! Nelatu is a chief, and *must* be heard!"

"Well, then, go on."

"You once said you were my friend. Nelatu tears your friendship from his breast and casts it to the wind! You are an assassin—a thief! What answer do you make?"

"I make none."

"You are right; nothing can be said to palliate the crime of falsehood, murder, and robbery! Come along with me."

"Indeed! Where to?"

"To our chief—to Wacora."

"A prisoner?"

"Yes."

"And who is to take me?"

"I will."

"You!" retorted Rody, with a sneer.

"Yes; your life was in my hands but a minute ago. You live only because I would not kill you in my sister's presence. Your very slave has proved false to you. You are in my power; Wacora shall pass sentence on you, and that sentence will be death!"

With a bound Warren rushed at Nelatu, who, suddenly dropping his rifle, grappled with him.

A terrible struggle ensued.

The young men were about equally matched in size and strength, while each knew that it was a contest for life or death.

Warren, by his unexpected onset, had at first some advantage over his antagonist; but the Indian speedily recovered it by his great power of endurance.

All feeling of pity had vanished from his breast.

He had intended to take him a prisoner; he would now kill him.

He made several unsuccessful efforts to draw his tomahawk; whilst Warren, inspired by the certainty that death would be the result, strove to his utmost to prevent him from wielding the weapon.

Long did they continue the struggle without either speaking a word. Their heavy breathing, as they rolled over and over on the grass, was the only audible sound.

Nelatu at length succeeded in getting his antagonist under him, and with one arm strove to hold him, whilst with the other he groped for his tomahawk.

At this moment Warren made a superhuman effort, threw the Indian off, and, with the speed of lightning, snatched his rifle from the ground.

Nelatu had stumbled as he was thrown off, and lay sprawling upon the earth.

Another instant and he would have had a bullet through his body.

Was it an echo that answered the cocking of the rifle held in Rody's hand?

That was the last thought that crossed Warren Rody's mind.

The next moment he was a corpse!

A bullet had pierced his brain!

It came from Maracota's gun, who had arrived upon the ground at the moment of Nelatu's fall.

Before either of the two Indians could speak a word, a piercing cry echoed in upon their ears, a girl came gliding through the bushes, and flung herself prostrate over the body.

It was Sansuta!

The air was filled with her lamentations as she kissed the cold forehead of Warren Rody, and with a thousand endearing terms endeavoured to recall him to life.

Nelatu approached and gently raised her from the ground.

He was about to address her, but he started back in horror, as he caught the expression of her face.

Her wild, starting eyes, with that unmeaning smile upon her lips, told the sad tale.

Her reason had departed!

---

# CHAPTER XXVIII.

### THE STRUGGLE IN THE STOCKADE.

N that same night the Indians, led by Wacora, stormed the stockade upon the hill.

The combat proved long and desperate, but the place was at length taken.

Bravely as the settlers fought, they had a foe to deal with implacable and determined.

As fast as the red warriors fell in the attack, others took their places, and from out the darkness legions seemed to rise to avenge the deaths of their fallen comrades.

The white women loaded the rifles, stood by their brothers and husbands, assisting them in the fearful strife.

But valour availed not; the settlers were doomed.

Never had Elias Rody been seen to greater advantage.

He seemed ubiquitous, cheering and inspiring the men around him.

Many who had condemned him till then gave him credit for his undoubted bravery.

He seemed to bear a charmed life, and was seen wherever bullets whistled, unharmed and undaunted!

All his hopes on earth were centred in successfully maintaining himself; and that strong physical courage which he undoubtedly possessed, stimulated by his frightful responsibility, made him for the moment heroic.

"OH, SPARE HER; TAKE MY LIFE INSTEAD."

His daughter, the gentle Alice, showed herself equally brave.

She took under her care the wounded men—she who, at any other time, would have fainted at the sight of blood—bound up the ghastly wounds, and stood on that dreadful night by more than one deathbed, calm and courageous, upheld by the sustaining idea.

But what availed courage and devotion against numbers?

The stockade was at length carried, and, after it, the house, which was instantly given to the flames.

A horrible carnage ensued amongst those who, unable to fly, were left to the besiegers' fury.

The worst passions were displayed in their worst forms, and helplessness pleaded in vain to hearts steeled with revenge.

The moon's rays lighted up a fearful scene.

Corpses of Indians and settlers, with their wives and children, strewed the ground of the enclosure!

The glare of the burning house added to the horror of the sight.

Some few of the colonists fled across the country, pursued by their relentless foes.

Though a small number escaped with life, many perished in their flight.

With revengeful cries the Indians sought for Elias Rody, but failed to find him.

Had he, too, escaped?

It seemed so, for nowhere could his body be discovered among the slain.

His daughter had also disappeared.

But half of their revenge seemed accomplished, and Wacora felt that with Rody alive, his uncle's death was not yet avenged.

In vain did he send warrior after warrior in search of the missing man.

All returned with the same answer.

The White Chief was not to be found!

Enraged at being thus baffled in his revenge, Wacora called his straggling forces together, and returned with them to the Indian camp.

After their departure there was profound stillness within the stockade, more awful from contrast with the battle there so late raging.

The dead were left to repose in peace.

For a long time this stillness continued unbroken.

Then from afar sounds began to be heard, gradually drawing nearer and nearer.

It was the howling of the gaunt Florida wolves as they scented a rich repast.

Ere long they could be seen skulking through the enclosure, and quarrelling over the corpses upon the plain. Above them, with shadowy wings, the vultures hovered, waiting to come in for their share of the spoil.

The moon sank in the sky, and drew a pall over the dreadful sight.

At intervals a flickering tongue of flame shooting up from the expiring embers of the burnt house, imparted a weird aspect to the scene, lighting it up only to display its ghastly horrors.

\* \* \* \* \*

Where was Elias Rody?

He had proved deceitful to the last.

Wacora and his warriors had sought him everywhere, but had failed to find him.

For all that he was near.

In the last attack made by the red-men he had been wounded—not se-verely, but sufficiently to make him feel faint and giddy. He knew that he could no longer hope for success, and deter-mined, if possible, to save his own life while there was a chance.

Amidst the smoke and confusion he found no difficulty in withdrawing from the combat. Remembering a species of cellar he had caused to be dug in the rear of the house, he staggered towards it, and reached it unobserved.

He paused before entering.

A thought of Alice arrested him— the thought of the hopelessness of saving her, and tottering forward, half blinded by his own blood, he descended the steps of the cellar, at the bottom of which he fell insensible to the floor.

The yells of the victorious Indians, the glare of the burning mansion, the shrieks of the wounded and the agoni-sing wail of defenceless women and chil-dren as they committed their souls to Heaven, Elias Rody, though the cause of all this, heard nothing of.

Beneath his own burning house, mi-raculously sheltered by some huge tim-bers which had fallen over the excava-tion, he lay for a long time insensible to thought as to feeling.

When he at length recovered con-sciousness, and crawled forth from his concealment, the sun had risen, lighting up the ruined pile.

He shuddered at the sight.

He suffered a thousand deaths in the contemplation of the horrors his mad selfishness had caused.

Bitter remorse, stronger than his shattered physical frame could endure, gnawed at his heart.

But it was selfish remorse for all that.

Here was vengeance for Oluski, had the chief only been alive to witness it.

Too weak to get away from the spot, Rody groaned in the bitterness of his spirit.

"Ten thousand times may I be ac-cursed for all this! Fool—blind, in-fatuated fool—that I have been. Every aspiration might have been gratified, every hope fulfilled, had not my impa-tience blinded me against caution. May the fiend of darkness overtake these red——"

How long this tirade of blasphemous repentance of his villany might have lasted it is impossible to say.

It was stopped, however, by a phy-sical pain, and with a faint voice he cried—

"Water! water!"

Blood there was in plenty around him, but not one drop of water.

Others had yelled for it through the long, dreadful night, as agonisingly as he, but had been answered by the same solemn silence.

*They* had died in their agony.

Why should not he?

"Well, then, let death come! The full accumulation of mortal torment has fallen on myself; it cannot be greater!"

Wrong in this, as in everything else.

See! Skulking along the brow of the hill, stooping over and examining corpse after corpse, with a look of de-moniac joy upon his hideous features, something in human shape, and yet scarce a man, appears.

Horror of horrors! he is robbing the dead.

Rody saw him not, for he had again fainted.

With a harsh voice, rivalling the vulture's croak, the skulker continued his hideous task.

"Ha! ha! ha!" chuckled he to himself, "there am nice pickings after all for dis chile, boaf from de bodies of white man and de red. Bress de chances what set 'em agin each oder! Oh, but de ole nigger am glad—so glad! But where am he?—where am he? If dis chile don't find him, why den dis work ain't more den half done!"

Diligently did Crookleg, for it was he, continue to search, turning over dead bodies, snatching some bauble from their breasts, and so passing on to others, as if still unsatisfied.

For whom was he seeking?

As he proceeded in his work, a voice that came from among a heap of ruins, was heard feebly calling for "Water!"

The negro started on hearing it, sending forth a shout of triumph.

He had recognised it as the voice of Elias Rody, the man for whom he had been searching.

As the latter recovered consciousness, he saw a hideous face close to his own, that caused him to start up, at the same time uttering a cry of horror.

---

# CHAPTER XXIX.

### AN EXULTING FIEND.

 "HAS found you, has I?"

"Crookleg!"

"Yes, it am Crookleg."

"A drop of water, for the love of God; a drop of water!"

"If de whole place war a lake, dis chile wouldn't sprinkle your parched lips with a drop out ob it."

"What do you mean, Crookleg?"

"Ha! the time I been waitin' for has come at last. It hab been long, but it am come! Do you know whar your son Warren am?"

"Thank Heaven! away from this, and in safety."

"Ha! ha! ha! Safe; yes, he am safe enough wid a big bullet through his brain!"

Elias Rody, with an effort, raised himself into a sitting posture, and glared upon the speaker.

"Dead!"

"Yes, dead; and it war me dat bro't him to it. Ha! ha! ha!"

"Who are you? Has hell let loose its fiends to mock me?"

"Perhaps it have. Who am I? Don't you know me yet, Rody—*Massa* Rody?"

"No, devil! I know you not. My

son dead—oh, God! what have I done to deserve all this?"

"What hab you done? What hab you not done? You hab done ebery ting that de black heart ob a white man do, and de day of reck'nin' am come at last. So you don't know me, don't you?"

"Away, fiend, and let me die in peace!"

"In peace—no; you shall die as you hab made oders live—in pain! When you can't hear dis nigga's voice plainly, he'll hiss it in at your ear, so it may reach your infernal soul, in de last minutes of you life?"

"Who—who are you?"

"I am Reuben, de son of Esther."

"Esther!"

"Yes, Esther, your father's slave. You was de cause ob her death. Do you know me now?"

Rody groaned.

"Dey called me Crookleg, kase I was lame. Who made me lame?"

Still no answer.

"It war you dat put de ball in my leg for sport, when you war a boy, an' I war de same. I have been close to you for years, but you didn't know me. I war too mean—too much below de notice of a proud gentleman like you. But I hab a good memory, and de oath I'd taken to be even wid ye, am kept. My mother war a slave, but she war my mother for all dat, an' if I war a black man, I war still a human bein', although you and de likes of you didn't think so. Do you know me now?"

Rody uttered not a word.

"When I war forced to limp away from your father's plantation, I war but a boy, but de boy had de same hate for de cruel massa dat de lame nigga hab now for Elias Rody. Days and years hab pass since den, but de hate war kept hot as ever; and I'se happy now when I knows dat de dyin' planter am at de mercy of de mean slave. Don't be skear'd. I wouldn't lift dis hand to help you eider die or live. All I'se a goin' to do is to sit hyar an' watch ober you till you am cold and stiff. Every flutter your wicked soul makes to get free from your ugly body, will be a joy to me!"

"Oh, devil!" exclaimed the wounded man in the depth of his agony.

"Debbil! Yes, I is a debbil, and you has made me one!"

The negro, as he said this, knelt down by Rody's side and thrust his face close up to that of the dying man, while a demoniac joy lit up his horrid features.

And he continued to gaze upon his victim until the grey shadow of dissolution stole over his countenance, the senses wandered, and the once bright eyes were becoming dimmed with the film of death.

At last a scream burst from the lips of the dying man, followed by words of piteous appeal.

"Ha—help—water—water! My soul's on fire! Devils—demons! Away—away! Let me go! Unloose your burning hands from my heart! Unloose—ah, horror!"

The cries ceased.

Elias Rody was dead!

Remorselessly did the negro glare upon his expiring enemy as he uttered these last frantic speeches, and when, at last, the spirit had passed away, he bounded to his feet and began to exult over his now unconscious victim.

At this moment another personage appeared upon the scene.

At some little distance from the spot a man, leaning upon his rifle, stood taking a mournful survey of the smoking ruins.

He had been for some time ignorant that any living being but himself was upon the hill.

His attention was now called to Crookleg, who, assured of his enemy's death, could no longer restrain his immense joy, but was giving vent to it in cries and fantastic caperings.

"Ho, ho—dead! It am 'plendid sport to de ole nigga! Only to tink dat dis poor ole lame darkey hab been de cause ob a war 'tween the whites and the redskins! Ha, ha, ha! it am most too good to be believed! But it am true—it am true!"

As the monstrous creature concluded the speech, he was seen to spring suddenly into the air and fall flat upon his face—a corpse!

A long hunting knife had penetrated his back!

"There, ye black hound! If you have been the cause of one war, you'll never have a hand in another. I swore not to fight agin my own blood, nor to take part agin the redskins, but black blood don't count in my bargain!"

Saying this, Cris Carrol drew his blade from the negro's body and coolly sauntered away from the spot.

---

## CHAPTER XXX.

### ROBBED OF HIS REVENGE.

ACORA, after reaching the camp, dismissed his warriors, and entered his tent alone.

The remainder of that night he passed in meditation.

Was it the influence of the white blood flowing in his veins that made him think of the slaughter he had directed and taken part in?

The heroic chief, still decked in the war paint of his father's race, as he reviewed the events of the past few hours, could not restrain himself from shuddering.

His mother's spirit seemed to hover around him; her eyes sad and reproachful; her heart heavy.

"They were the people of my race, and so of yours, that you have immolated on the throne of your vengeance."

So seemed it to say!

His head sank upon his breast. He sighed heavily.

Long he continued in his gloomy abstraction; his thoughts deeper than plummet ever sounded.

The weary hours of night crept slowly past, and yet he stirred not.

Fears and forebodings filled his warrior's heart.

"I have done all for the best," muttered he to himself. "Witness it, thou Great Spirit; all for the best. For the future of my father's race I have closed my heart to pity. It was not for present vengeance alone that I urged on the wild people to the slaughter. It was that they might then begin the great work of regeneration, assured in their strength, and conscious of their invincibility."

Like all high-strung natures, Wacora was subject to fits of despondency.

With want of action this had come upon him. The excitement over, gloomy doubt had succeeded to bright hope.

The sun was high in the heavens ere he could bestir himself, and shake off such thoughts. He at length made the effort, and emerged from his tent to consult with the principal warriors of his tribe.

As he stepped forth, he perceived Maracota slowly approaching.

In an instant the slumbering passion of hate was awakened; he saw in the young Indian's eye that he had news to communicate.

"Speak! have you found him?"

"Yes, he is found."

"I mean Warren Rody. Make no error, Maracota—tell me, is it Warren Rody you have found?"

"He has been found."

"Then all is well. Quick! bring him to me. Let me look upon this dog of a pale-face!"

Maracota made no answer, but stood silent.

"Do you hear me? Bring the dog before me. My eyes hunger for a sight of his craven countenance—I would see his white-livered face of fear—watch his trembling frame as he stands in my presence!"

Still Maracota did not speak.

"By the Great Spirit, Maracota, why do you not go for him? Why do you not answer me?"

"Maracota dreads your anger."

"You an Indian warrior, and afraid! What do you mean?"

"That I have disobeyed your commands——"

"Ha! wretch! I understand. You found him, but he escaped."

"Not that——"

"What is it then? Speak, did he defy you? Was he too powerful? Then summon our warriors, and if it cost the life of every Indian in Florida, I swear he shall be captured. Answer me, or I shall do you mischief."

"Maracota deserves punishment."

The young chief, now fully aroused to anger, cast a significant look at his subordinate; he could scarce refrain from striking him to the ground, and it was with an effort that he resumed speech.

"No more mystery. Speak! where is he?"

"Dead."

Wacora made a bound towards the speaker, as he cried. "Did *you* kill him?"

"I did."

Maracota fearlessly stood to await the stroke of the upraised tomahawk.

It fell, but not on the Indian's skull.

Wacora flung his weapon on the grass.

"Wretch!" he cried, "you have robbed me of my revenge. May the arm that took that man's life hang palsied by your side for ever! May—oh, curse you—curse you!"

Maracota's head fell upon his breast. He dared not meet his chief's angry glance—more dreaded than the blow of his hatchet.

For some moments there was silence; whilst Wacora paced to and fro like a tiger in its cage.

## CHAPTER XXXI.

### A SAD SPECTACLE.

FTER a time the enraged chief, pausing in his steps, stood by the side of the silent warrior.

"Tell me how it happened," he said, apparently becoming calmer. "Tell me all."

Maracota related the circumstances as they had happened.

"It was to save Nelatu's life that you fired upon the monster?"

"It was."

"And he—where is Nelatu?"

"He is close by. See, they come this way."

As Wacora looked in the direction indicated, he perceived his two cousins approaching.

The beautiful maiden, now wan and sad, seemed absorbed in the contemplation of some wild flowers which she held in her hand. There were others wreathed in her hair.

In this manner had she been conducted to the camp.

Nelatu turned to his sister, put his arm in hers, and was about to lead her off, when a man rushed into the presence of the chief, crying out as they approached—

"Good news! The body of the white chief, Rody, has been found, and——"

The warning gesture had been lost upon the impatient speaker.

It was too late now. Sansuta had heard the fated name.

Casting from her the flowers she had been trifling with, she uttered shriek upon shriek, running wildly and beseechingly backwards and forwards, from her brother to her cousin, who both stood spellbound with surprise and grief.

"Where have you hid him? Give him to me? You shall not kill him; no—no—no! I say you shall not hurt him! Warren! Warren! 'tis Sansuta calls. Murderers! He never injured you. Take my life—not his! Warren! Warren! Oh, do not keep him from me. See, that is his blood upon your hands—his eyes are closed in death!

"It is you wretches that have murdered him. No, no; stand back—I would not have you touch me whilst your hands are red with his blood. Back! back! I will find him!—No, you shall kill me first!—I will find Warren Rody!

"Help, help! Save me from his murderers!"

With renewed screams of agony that struck horror into the listeners' hearts, the girl, eluding their grasp, darted away into the forest.

At a signal from Wacora, Nelatu started in pursuit.

"May the lightnings blast all who have brought about this! Fool that I was just now to feel pity for the pale-faces; nothing that revenge can accomplish will make up for this. Here I swear to take vengeance far more terrible—vengeance to which that of last night shall be but a mockery?"

With these words the young chief hastened away from the spot, followed by Maracota and the messenger who had brought the news of Rody's death.

---

## CHAPTER XXXII.

"SPARE HER! SPARE HER!"

HE opportunity of this vengeance was already close at hand.

Within the space enclosed by the Indian tents, under guard of some warriors, stood a group of pale-face prisoners.

It consisted of several men, and among them a young girl.

Wacora stopped on perceiving the group.

His features were illumined with a savage joy.

One of the chiefs, advancing, reported their having been captured while attempting to escape through the adjoining forest.

"What's to be done with them?" he asked.

"They shall die by torture!"

"The girl?"

"She, too, shall die! Who is she?"

"I don't know."

Turning to Maracota, he propounded a similar question.

Maracota was equally ignorant of the person of the captive.

The chief ordered her to be brought before him.

With an undaunted step, although

evidently suffering from debility and sorrow, the girl allowed herself to be led along.

Once in Wacora's presence, with a modest courage, she gazed into his face.

" Who are you ?" he asked.

" Your prisoner."

" When were you captured ?"

" About two hours ago."

" You were trying to escape ?"

" I was."

" Your companions—who are they ?"

" I know nothing of them, except that they are people belonging to the settlement. They were kind to me, and endeavoured to help me in my escape."

" You know your doom ?"

She answered, sadly—

" I expect no mercy."

Wacora, struck with this reply, felt an interest in the courageous girl which he could not account for.

" You have been taught to think of the red-man as a remorseless savage ?"

" Not as remorseless, only as revengeful."

" Then you acknowledge that we have just cause for revengeful feelings ?"

" I did not say so."

" But you implied it."

" All men have enemies. The truly great are the only ones who can forego revenge."

" But savages must act according to their instincts."

" Savages—yes. But men who know right from wrong should act by their judgment."

" If I spared your life, you would still consider me a savage."

" My life is nothing to me. All those I loved are now dead."

" Your mother ?"

" She died when I was a child."

" Your father ?"

" Was killed last night."

Wacora seemed lost in thought as he said, half aside—

" So young, and yet with no fear of death !"

The young girl overheard the muttered soliloquy, and made answer—

" To the unhappy death is welcome."

" Unhappy ?"

" I have told you that all I love are dead."

" Yet death is terrible.

" Your name ?"

" Alice Rody."

With a cry of fiendish delight, Wacora grasped the maiden's arm.

" You, the daughter of that accursed man—the daughter of that demon in human form ! Then, by the Great Spirit above us ! by the ashes of my ancestors, you shall die ! My own hand shall inflict the blow."

As he uttered these words, he drew a knife from his belt, and was on the point of sheathing it in her heart, when his arm was seized, and a voice, full of agony, vibrated in his ear—

" Spare her !—oh ! spare her ! Take my life instead."

" Nelatu !"

" Yes, Nelatu ; your cousin—your slave, if you will—only spare her life !"

" You forget her name."

" No, no ; I know it but too well."

" You forget that her father has been the accursed cause of all this misery ?"

" No ; I remember that too."

" Then you are insane thus to beg for her life. She must die !"

" I am not insane.  Oh, Wacora, on my knees I implore you to spare her !"

" Rise, Nelatu ; the son of Oluski should not bend his knee to man.  At your intercession, her life is spared !"

Nelatu rose from the ground.

" You are indeed our chief, Wacora. Your heart is open and generous."

" Stay, yet, before you mistake me. I give you her life ;—but ' an eye for an eye.'  She shall suffer what Sansuta has suffered ; spare her life, but not her honour."

" Wacora !"

" I have said it.  Here"—turning to the assembled warriors who had been amazed witnesses of the scene—" this is the child of our enemy, Elias Rody.  I have, at Nelatu's entreaty, spared her life ; I bestow her upon the tribe ; do with her as you will."

Nelatu leaped before the advancing braves.

" Back !" he cried.  " The first who lays hands upon her dies !"

Wacora gazed upon his cousin.

In his breast rage contended with wonder.

" Heed him not ; he is insane."

" No, not insane."

" Speak ; what then ?"

" I love her !  I love her !"

The young girl, who had stood like a statue through all the previous scene, gave a start, and cowering to the ground, buried her face in her hands.

To Wacora the words of Nelatu were no less surprising.

Turning to the shrinking maiden, he said—

" You have heard what Nelatu says ? He loves you."

She murmured, faintly—

" I hear."

" He loves you.  Wacora, too, has loved.  That love has been trampled upon, and by your wretch of a brother ; yet still it shall plead for Nelatu.  His request is granted.  You are spared both life and honour, but must remain a prisoner.  Conduct her hence !"

" And these ?" asked a warrior, pointing to the other prisoners.

Wacora's heart, touched for an instant by his cousin's pleading, as well as by Alice Rody's heroic bearing, became again hardened.

He replied—

" They must die !  Not by the torture, but at once.  Let them be shot !"

The brave fellows, disdaining to sue for mercy, were led away from the spot.

Soon after he heard several shots that came echoing from the woods.

His captives had been released from all earthly care.

"IN THE DARKEST CORNER OF THE HUT HE PERCEIVED THE FACE OF A YOUNG GIRL,"

NO. 7.

# CHAPTER XXXIII.

### RUIN AMONG THE RUINS.

HE Indians' encampment near Tampa Bay was broken up.

The women and children, attended by a few warriors, had departed for the town.

Alice Rody, a prisoner, went along with them.

Wacora, Nelatu, and the rest of the tribe, joined others of their race in the war which was now rapidly spreading over the whole peninsula.

For a time the Seminole tribe led a wandering life.

The varying successes or defeats of the protracted contest entailed upon them both vigilance and activity.

It was, therefore, only occasionally that the cousins were enabled to visit the town in which their people permanently resided.

Sansuta had now seldom any relapses of her fits of violent madness.

She was silent and melancholy, and wandered about wrapped in her own bewildered thoughts.

Alice, although a prisoner, was suffered to come and go as it pleased her.

Nelatu's love for the pale-faced maiden made no progress.

A wan smile was all the reward the Indian youth received for his patient devotion.

He felt that his passion was hopeless, but still he nursed it.

To Sansuta, Alice indeed proved a guardian angel.

At first the Indian girl repelled the tender solicitude expressed by the white maiden, and with an alarmed look seemed to dread even her voice.

In time, however, won by the magic of kindness, she sought the company of the captive, and in her presence seemed happy.

Often they would stroll away from the town, and in some quiet spot pass hours together—Alice in silent thought, Sansuta in such childish employment as stringing beads, or making baskets with the flowers and tendrils of the wild vine.

A favourite haunt with them both was the old fort.

Amongst its ruins they would seat themselves in silence, each with her own thoughts.

And thus was their time tranquilly passed, and was succeeded by a temporary calm.

The pale-faces had abandoned the smaller settlements and detached plantations, and in the neighbouring towns awaited the arrival of the Government troops on their way to prosecute the campaign throughout the whole peninsula.

The Indians had sought their respective rendezvous, there to mature plans for a more perfect organisation.

Nelatu and Wacora had returned home, for such was the title Wacora now gave to the place where Oluski's tribe had their permanent residence.

The exigencies of the contest had compelled the withdrawal of his warriors from his father's town, and the two tribes, Oluski's and his own, had become fused into one powerful community.

The chief's feeling towards his captive had undergone a marked change.

He no longer wished to harm her, and had she demanded from him her liberty, he would have granted it freely.

Of what use is liberty to the homeless?

Alice Rody had become careless of her freedom—nay, in a manner, preferred her captivity to the uncertainty of an unknown future, where no kindred awaited her return, no friend stood expectant to receive her.

A sense of security—almost contentment—had stolen into her heart.

Time had done much to assuage the terrible sorrow from which she had suffered.

It was a wonderful transformation to the once high-spirited girl, who had shown such energy and fortitude in the midst of danger.

So thought the young chief, Wacora.

To Nelatu it was a negative happiness. She had not the energy to chide his ardent devotion, but submitted to it passively, without bestowing the slightest encouragement.

One lovely evening Sansuta, conducted by Alice, strolled to the ruined fort.

Arrived there, Sansuta proceeded to embroider a pouch she had commenced to make.

Alice, seated on a fragment of a stone, watched her companion's trivial employment.

As the Indian girl nestled close to the pale-faced maiden, she seemed on the point of fainting.

She had grown thinner during the last few weeks, and her hollow cheeks were tinted with a hectic flush.

"Rest your head on my lap, Sansuta."

As Alice spoke, she gently caught the poor girl in her arms.

"I am tired, oh, so tired!" said Sansuta.

"You must not walk so far as this another time. We must seek some place nearer to the town."

The Indian girl did not appear to heed her, but commenced singing softly to herself.

She paused abruptly in her song, and looked up into her companion's face.

"Last night I dreamed I was in another land, walking along a footpath. It was strewn with lovely flowers. On both sides were beautiful creeping plants, over which bright butterflies sailed. There were two birds—such birds—their plumage of silver and gold. I heard music. Was it in the land of the Great Spirit? Do you think it was?"

"Who knows? It might have been!"

"There I met my father. Not stern, as our warriors are, but sad and weeping. Why did he weep?"

Alice was silent. Her own tears hindered her from making answer to the artless question.

"When I saw him weeping, I too, wept, and kissed him. He spoke kindly to me; but why did he weep?"

Still no answer from her listening companion.

"Then I dreamt—no, I cannot remember what else I dreamt—yet there was some one else there. I seemed to know his face, too; but a great storm arose, and all became dark, and I grew frightened. What was that?" asked the poor Indian girl.

"Alas! Sansuta, I cannot read my own dreams, far less yours."

But Sansuta had already forgotten her question, and was again singing softly to herself.

Presently she stopped once more, and putting both arms around Alice's neck, murmured that she was tired.

The pale-faced maiden kissed her, and, as she did so, the tears from her eyes fell on Sansuta's cheeks.

"Why do you weep? Who has injured you?"

Had Alice framed her thoughts into words she would have answered, the whole world; but, instead, she only replied to her companion with gentle endearments, and, at length, caressed her into a gentle sleep.

It was a beautiful tableau for a painter to delineate—beautiful—but at the same time sadly impressive.

A young Indian chief, who had been a silent witness to it, must have thought so, by the sigh that escaped him, as he turned his face away.

Wacora was the chief who thus sighed.

---

# CHAPTER XXXIV.

### STRANGE CHANGES.

ACORA'S love for Sansuta had long since changed into pity.

A new feeling now possessed his heart.

A new love had arisen from the ashes of the past.

Alice Rody was the object!

He had at first been struck with admiration at her courage; afterwards he had witnessed her discretion and tenderness, and then noted her beauty.

His thoughts, thus stirred, soon ripened into a passion far stronger than respect.

Pity and love had exchanged places within his bosom.

He and his captive had done the same.

The girl was free; her gaoler had become her prisoner.

This new phase of feeling was not accomplished suddenly.

It grew silently and slowly, but surely.

One thought troubled Wacora.

It was Nelatu's admiration for Alice Rody.

He saw that she cared not for his cousin, but he forebore to urge his suit, out of compassion for Sansuta's brother.

His love, therefore was speechless, and his captive was unconscious of it.

But what of her?

She, too, was changed.

By one of those marvellous transformations of which the human heart is capable, Alice Rody not only became reconciled to her residence among the Indians, but even found much that interested her, even to the awakening of pleasant thoughts.

Many of the Seminoles were, as has been stated, well educated, and with education had come the usual chastening influence.

This was especially true of the young chief Wacora, and she had not failed to observe it.

Her first reflection was what he might have been had he been brought up amongst her own race, for although she had not been told of his mother being a white woman, she did not doubt that he had white blood in his veins.

What might not a man of his intelligence, chivalric courage, and purity of thought have become in a society where civilisation would have developed all these mental qualities?

The question was a natural one when viewing only the advantages which high culture presented; but its obverse was unfavourable, when considering that civilisation is often an approach to barbarism through selfishness and rapacity.

She answered the query herself, and favourably for him. This mental questioning, once commenced, did not pause, but went on to farther consideration of the character of the young chief.

His thoughtfulness seemed as much sprung from regret at the compulsory warfare he was waging against her race, as the noble enthusiasm with which his soul was filled.

The heart of woman easily yielded its admiration to an enthusiast!

The motive may be condemned, but the spiritual essence of thought that prompts to action still remains to be admired.

It will then be seen that the first abhorrence had given place to interest; and interest had ripened into—

Into what?

There was no answer to that question. As it came before Alice Rody's mind she evaded it, and strove calmly to consider Wacora as her captor.

But it soon seemed impossible to look upon him in this light.

No *preux chevalier* could be more courteous in his bearing—no prince more calmly conscious of his own birthright.

His was of the oldest patent. Whether thinking so or not, he was one of Nature's noblemen.

A few months had wrought these marvellous changes in the personages of our tale, and upon Wacora's sudden departure to the scene of war, both he and his captive felt a strange void in their hearts unaccountable, because novel.

Nelatu, whose hope of winning the regard of the pale-faced maiden had sunk into a calm state of despair, departed with his cousin, hoping that in the field of battle he might find a still calmer rest.

His fate, wrapped in the dark mystery of the future, was veiled from him.

## CHAPTER XXXV.

### A PEACEFUL WARNING.

HE summer had waned into autumn.

With the changing season came also a change over the hapless Indian maiden, Sansuta.

Her weakness, which had been continually increasing, was now so great that she could no longer stray with Alice to their favourite haunts.

The poor girl's form had wasted away, and her features become shrunken.

Her dark, lustrous eyes alone seemed to retain their vitality.

All her former violence had disappeared, and a change had also made itself manifest in her mental condition.

Now and then she had lucid moments of thought, during which she would shed torrents of tears on Alice's shoulder; only with the return of her malady would she appear happy and at peace.

Towards sunset of a lovely day the two girls sat together at the door of Sansuta's dwelling.

"See!" said the Indian girl, "the flowers are closing, the birds have gone into the deep forest. I have been ex-pecting some one, but he has not come yet. Do you know who it is?"

"No, I do not."

"'Tis Warren. Why do you start and tremble? He will not hurt you. Who was it you thought I meant?"

"I cannot tell, dear Sansuta."

"No one but him—I think of him always, although," she added, lowering her voice to a whisper, "I dare not call his name. I'm afraid to do that, I'm afraid of my brother Nelatu, and my cousin Wacora. Why does the sun look so fiery? It is the colour of blood, blood, blood! That red colour, is it on *your* hands, too? Ah, no! *You* are no murderer!"

"Hush, Sansuta! you are excited."

"Ah, yonder sun! Do you know that I feel as if it were the last time I should ever see it set. See, there are dark lines across the sky, ribbed with bands of black clouds. It is the last day, the last day——"

"I see nothing, only the approach of night."

"But you hear something. Don't you hear the spirits singing their death march over Oluski's grave? He was my father—I hear it. It is a summons. It is for me. I must go."

"Go? Where?"

"Far away. No; it is no use clasping me to your heart. It is not Sansuta's body that will leave you—it is her spirit. In the happy hunting grounds I shall meet with him——"

A few moments after she became tranquil; but the lucid interval succeeded, and hot tears coursed down her hollow cheeks.

Again her mind wandered, and for two or three hours, refusing to enter the house, she sat muttering to herself the same fancies.

Alice could but sit beside her and listen.

Now and then she sought to soothe her, but in vain.

By and bye Sansuta's voice grew faint.

She seemed to lean heavier on the arm of her pale-faced friend, and the lustre of her eye gradually became dimmer.

The change was alarming, and Alice would have risen and called for help, but an imploring glance from Sansuta prevented her.

"Don't leave me," she murmured.

Her voice was changed; she had recovered reason, and her companion perceived it.

"Do not leave me. I shall not detain you long. I know you now—have known you it seems for years. I know all, for there is peace in my heart towards all, even to those who took his life. Forgiveness has come back with reason, and my last prayers shall be that they who made Sansuta unhappy may be forgiven!"

She spoke in so low a voice that it was with difficulty her companion could hear what she said.

"Kiss me, Alice Rody! Speak to me! Let me hear you say that Sansuta was your friend!"

"Was—is my friend!"

"No—let me say was, for I am about to leave you. The time is come; I am ready! My last prayer is 'Pity and forgiveness! Pity and——'"

By the gentle motion of her lips she appeared to be praying.

That motion ceased, and with it her unhappy life!

Alice still continued to hold her in her arms long after her soul had passed into Eternity!

## CHAPTER XXXVI.

### THE BURNT SHANTY.

HE ghost of Crookleg did not in any way disturb Cris Carrol, either sleeping or awake.

The worthy backwoodsman believed that he had done a highly meritorious action in for ever disposing of that malevolent individual.

"The infernal black skunk, to be cuttin' his capers over the bodies of brave men who had laid down their lives in a war he, and sich as he, brought about! It were no more nor an act of justice to send him to everlastin' perdition, and, if I never done a more valyable thing to society than stickin' three inches of cold steel atween his two shoulder-blades, I think I desarves the thanks of the hul community."

This consolation Cris indulged in whenever he thought of that terrible episode upon Tampa hill.

He had returned a few days after the massacre and had found the dead decently buried.

Wacora had commanded it to be done.

The charred ruins of Rody's house, however, recalled the memory of that eventful night.

For some time after his last visit to Tampa Bay, Cris Carrol had not been seen.

Neither the pale-faces nor the redskins had been able to discover his whereabouts.

In truth the backwoodsman was glad to get away from scenes where so much violence had been done to his feelings.

As he had said, he *couldn't* fight against the Indians, and he *wouldn't* take up arms against the whites.

"It ain't in human nature to shoot and stab one's own sort, even when they're in the wrong, unless they'd done somethin' agin oneself; an' that they hain't done, as regards me. I'll be eternally dog-goned if I think the red-skins are to blame for rising agin oppression and tyranny, which is what old Rody did to them, to say nothin' agin him now he's dead, but to speak the truth, and that's bad enough for him. No, they war not to blame for what they did, arter his conduct to them—the old cuss; who, bad as he war, had one redeemin' feature in his karactur, and that war his angeliferous darter. Where kin she have gone a hidin'?

"That puzzles this chile, it do."

Cris was unaware of Alice's capture and imprisonment.

As suddenly as he had taken departure from Tampa, Cris returned to the same neighbourhood.

He expected the war to be transferred to a more distant point, and wished still to keep out of the way.

"It's the durnedst fightin' I ever heard on," said he to himself; "first it's here, then it's there, and then it ain't nowhere; till it breaks out all over again where it was before, and they're as far off the end as I am from Greenland. Durn it, I never knowed nothin' like it."

On his return to Tampa, he found the country around altogether deserted.

Most of the buildings and the planter's house had been destroyed; even his own wretched hut had been burnt to the ground.

"This is what they call the fortun' of war, 'spose?" he remarked, as he stood gazing at the ruins. "Wal, it war a ramshackle crazy ole shanty anyhow, and I allers despised four walls an' a roof at the best o' times—still it war 'home.' Pshaw!" he added, after a moment's silence, "what have I to grow molloncholly about, over sich a place as this—calling it 'home,' when I still have the savannas to hunt over an' sleep upon? If thar's such a place as home for me, that's it, and no other."

For all his stoicism, the old hunter sighed as he turned from the blackened spot which marked the site of his former dwelling.

He paused at the bend of the road, where Crookleg had first met Nelatu, to gaze again at his ruined home.

Not only paused, but sat down upon the self-same rail that the negro had perched upon, and from gazing upon it, fell to reflecting.

So absorbed was he in his contemplation, that contrary to his usual custom, he took no note of the time, nor once removed his eyes from the subject of his thoughts.

He did not perceive the approach of a danger.

It came in the form of four individuals who had stealthily crept close to the spot where he was sitting.

Before he knew of their proximity, he was their prisoner.

"Red-skins!" he exclaimed, struggling to free himself.

His captors smiled grimly at his vain efforts.

"By the eternal! I'm fixed this time! Darn my stupid carcase for not havin' eyes set in the back o' the head. Wal, you may grin, old copperskins; it's your turn now—maybe it'll be mine next. What are you a-doin' now?"

Without deigning a reply, the Indians bound his arms securely behind him.

That done, they made signs to him to follow them.

"Wal, gentlemen," said Cris, "ye're about as silent a party as a man might wish to meet, darn me if you ain't. I'm comin'.

"Much obleeged to you for your escort, which I ked ha' done without. Thanks to your red-skin perliteness for nothin'. Go ahead; I kin walk without your helpin' me. Where are ye bound for?"

"To the chief," answered one of the men.

"The chief! What chief?"

"Wacora."

Cris uttered an emphatic oath.

"Wacora, eh? If that's the case, I reckon the days o' Cris Carrol air drawin' to a close. The fiercest and most vengeful cuss of them all, I've heard say. Lead on; I'll go along with ye willin', but not cheerful. If they kill me like a man, I'll not tremble in a jint; but if it's the torture—there, go ahead. Don't keep the party waitin'."

Brave heart as he was, he followed them with as bold and free a step to what he believed to be his death, as if he had been alone, and at liberty on the savanna.

The Indians, without exchanging a word, either among themselves or with their captive, proceeded as rapidly as possible in the direction of Oluski's town.

# CHAPTER XXXVII.

### DEATH AT THE STAKE.

T night they encamped in the forest.

Lighting no fires, lest the light might betray them to their enemies, they produced from their packs some dried meat and meal cake.

Cris did full justice to the humble fare, although he made rather a wry face at the gourd of spring water with which he was invited by his captors to wash down the frugal repast.

Mastering his aversion, he, however, managed to swallow a few mouthfuls.

Supper over, two of his captors wrapped themselves in their blankets, and immediately fell asleep.

The other two remained awake, watching him.

Carrol saw that any attempt to escape under the eyes of two Indians would be idle.

One he might have coped with, even unarmed as he was.

Two would be more than a match for him, and he knew that on the slightest alarm the sleeping men would awake, making it four to one.

With the philosophy of a stoic he threw himself upon the ground, and also fell asleep.

He awoke once in the night to find that his guards had been changed.

There was no better prospect of freedom than before.

" Durn them! they're bound to fix me, I kin see that plain enough. Besides, with these 'ternal all-fired thongs cuttin' into my elbows, what could I do?"

Apparently nothing, for with a muttered curse at his own stupidity, he again composed himself to slumber.

With the dawn of morning Cris and his captors continued their journey.

They made no other halt before reaching the town.

Carrol in vain tried to draw from them the reason of their unexpected presence at so great a distance from the residence of the tribe.

They gave him no satisfaction.

He discovered, however, that whatever errand they had been sent on, they had failed in accomplishing it, and his own capture began to be considered by him as a peace offering with which they intended to mollify Wacora's wrath at their want of success in the mission with which they had been charged.

"Wal," reflected he, " I suppose I'm in some poor devil's place; perhaps I mout take more pleasure in doing him this good turn if I only knowed who he is. No doubt he's got some folks as 'ud grieve over him, but there ain't a many as will fret over Cris Carrol, not as I know on—yes, all right! go ahead. Let's go whar glory waits us, ye catawampous scamps, you. Ah! four to one; if it had been two to one, or, at a pinch, three to one, I'd have tried it on, if it had cost me all I've got, and that's my life—yah! it's almost enough to make one turn storekeeper to think on't."

Unmoved by the taunts and jeers which Cris liberally bestowed upon them during the journey, the Indians continued to watch him narrowly.

It was about mid-day when they arrived at their destination.

On entering the Indian town Carrol was thrust into one of the houses, where he was left to await the order of Wacora as to his final disposition.

Four guards were kept over him, two inside the house, two without.

He expected immediate death, but he was left undisturbed for the rest of the day, and at night received some supper, consisting of dried meat, bread and water.

He was then permitted to pass the hours till morning as seemed best to him. He soon arranged his plans.

He wrapped the blanket that had been given him around his body, and in a few moments was in a sound slumber.

His sleep lasted until a hand upon his shoulder, along with a summons to awake, aroused him.

It was one of his guards of yesterday who addressed him.

" Come !"

" Is that you, old dummy ?" asked he, recognising the Indian. "I can't say I'm glad to see you, since you've broke in on the pleasantest dream I've had for a long time. But never mind; how shed you know that you war a doing it, you poor savage critter you, that don't know nothin' but to handle a tomahawk, and raise the hair off a human head ? What do you want with me now ?"

" The warriors are assembled !"

" Air they ? Wal, that's kind of them, only they needn't have put themselves out of the way to get up so early on my account; I could have waited."

" Come."

" Wal, I'm comin' ; d'ye think I'm afraid, durn ye ? D'ye think I'm afraid of you or all the warriors of your tribe, or of your chief, Wacora, either ?"

" Wacora is not here."

" Not here ! Where is he ?"

" I cannot answer the pale-face's questions. I come to bring you before the council."

" Wal, I'm ready to go afore the council."

As they were about to emerge from the house, a sudden idea seemed to strike Carrol, and he stopped his conductor.

" Say, friend, will you tell me one thing ?"

" Speak !"

" Whar ar we ?"

" At Oluski's town."

Carrol's face beamed with a sudden joy.

" And his son, Nelatu—is this his home ?"

" It is."

" Hurray ! Now, I dare say you wonder at my bein' struck all of a heap wi' delight. But I'll tell you one thing, red-skin—no offence, not knowin' your name—you and y'ur three partners have taken a most uncommon sight of trouble all for nothin'."

" What do you mean ?"

" Just this—go and tell Nelatu that Cris Carrol is the party as you sneaked up to and took prisoner, and arter that, streak it for your precious lives."

" Nelatu ?"

" Yes, Nelatu, he's a friend o' this ole coon, and one that'll prove himself so, too, in giving you skunks as took me a deal more nor you bargained for."

" Nelatu is not here."

" Not here ? Why, didn't you tell me just now that this war his father's town ?"

" I did ; but Nelatu is not here."

" Not now, perhaps ; but I s'pose he'll be here ?"

" He will not return for weeks."

Carrol's countenance fell.

" Then, dog-gone your skin, lead on ! I throw up the pack of cards now that the trump's out of them. 'Tis my luck, and it's the darndest luck I ever seed ; there's no standing agin it. I s'pose I must give in."

Without another word he followed his guards.

They entered the council chamber where the assembled warriors awaited them.

With his foot upon the threshold, his manner entirely changed from the light, jeering hilarity he had exhibited to that of a calm and dignified bearing.

He saw in an instant that he was foredoomed.

The stern expression of his judges told him as much.

The mock ceremonial of examination was proceeded with, and a vain attempt made to extract from him intelligence of the movements of the whites, especially of the numbers and disposition of the government troops, some of whom had by this time arrived in the peninsula.

His disdainful refusal to betray his own race did him no service.

True, he was already sentenced to die, but the manner of his death might inflict horror on him who had no fear of dying.

Though the questions were skilfully put to him, the old hunter saw through them all.

He did not, indeed, possess much knowledge of the military invasion; but had he been in the secret of the commanding officer himself, he could not have been more reticent in his replies.

Utterly foiled in their questions, the warriors played their last card, and with threats of the most terrible tortures, endeavoured to wring from his fears what his honour would not reveal.

Vain effort on their part.

Cris did, indeed, wince when they first spoke of torture; but recovering himself, he became more proudly defiant than before.

"Ye may shake my ole body with rackin' pains. I know you've got devil's inventions, and I don't deny but they're awful; but there's somethin' about me that ye can't make tremble, not if all the imps o' hell war yer slaves—that's my soul. It'll come out o' yer fiery ordeal as calm as it is now; and with its last thoughts it'll despise and dare ye! Cris Carrol arn't bin backwoods hunter for a matter goin' on forty year to be skeart at burning sticks or hot lead; and he'll die as he has lived, an honest man!"

A mingled murmur of admiration and anger ran through the assembled crowd, and it was evident that many of the warriors would have given their consent to his being set free.

There is something about TRUE courage which extorts admiration even from an enemy.

A hurried consultation took place among the head men in council.

It was speedily over, and the oldest of their number rose and pronounced sentence against the prisoner.

It was death by burning at the stake!

Cris Carrol was not surprised on hearing it.

The sentence had already lost half of its terror.

He had made up his mind that this would be his doom.

Only one word of response came from his lips.

"When?"

"To-morrow!" replied he who had pronounced judgment.

Without bestowing a glance upon those who had thus fixed the limit of his earthly career, the hunter strode from the council chamber with calm and measured steps.

As he passed out, the crowd made way for him, and many of the faces expressed admiration, some even pity.

The stoic bravery of the Indian is marvellous, and for him death has no terrors.

With them it is a sort of fatalism.

What they do not dread themselves, they make but light of in others.

For all that, they have the highest admiration for a man who dares meet death calmly.

In their eyes the white captive had assumed all the importance of a great warrior.

Yet was he an enemy, one of the race with whom they were at war, therefore he must die.

Thus strangely do civilization and barbarism meet on common ground.

# CHAPTER XXXVIII.

### THE SLEEPING DRAUGHT.

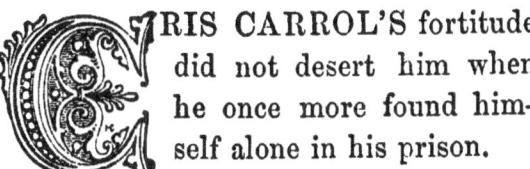RIS CARROL'S fortitude did not desert him when he once more found himself alone in his prison.

He was not wholly unmoved by the reflection that on the morrow he must die; for it was a death such as even a brave man might not meet bravely, but a lingering death by torture.

The hunter knew what this meant.

" A bullet ain't nothin'," said he to himself; " it's into yer body afore ye knows it, and if it's in your vitals, there's an end on it; but to stand up to be prodded with burning sticks requires philosophy a'most as much as this hyar chile have got. Dog-rot it, it won't bear thinkin' on, that it won't. But I'll be all-fired eternally if them fellows shall know how it hurts Cris Carrol! So let 'em do their worst, durn 'em!"

After this self-consoling soliloquy, he calmly went to work to make himself comfortable by laying his blanket on the bare ground, and improvising a pillow out of some logs that lay within reach.

As he handled the billets, a strange desire seized him.

It was to knock his guards' brains out and make a dash for liberty.

But a moment's reflection convinced him that the attempt at escape would be futile, the men outside being doubtless prepared to oppose his exit.

A disinclination to shed blood uselessly decided him, and he lay down composedly after lighting his pipe.

For some time he ruminated on his condition, puffing curls of smoke into the air, and watching them as they disappeared.

Once or twice he heard a scratching noise near the corner of the room, but it ceased almost as soon as he had noticed it.

At length, giving way to weariness, he composed himself to sleep, and before long, his loud snoring suggested to his guards that they might relax their vigilance.

They accordingly retired outside the door, after having assured themselves that his slumber was genuine.

There were still four of them, and they began chattering to each other, for a time forgetting their prisoner.

He was at length awakened by a gentle tug at his arm, which had to be repeated several times before it had the effect of arousing him.

In an instant he sat up.

"Eh?—what? By the etarnal——"

An admonition of silence checked him, and he surveyed, with an astonished countenance, the cause of his disturbance.

In the darkest corner of the hut he perceived an opening, through which the face of a young girl was visible.

He started on recognizing her.

"Hush!" she said, in a whisper. "Remember you are watched. Lie down again, listen; but say nothing. Ha! they are coming back!"

At these words the speaker withdrew, just in time, as two of the guards next moment re-entered the room.

They did not stay long.

The heavy snoring which Cris improvised for them disarmed them of suspicion.

The moment they were again gone, he turned his eyes towards the opening, and listened.

"Do you know me? Answer by a sign."

Cris nodded in the affirmative.

"You believe I am desirous to serve you?"

To this question he almost nodded his head off.

"Listen, then, and be careful to obey my instructions. This opening leads into the next house. The exit from it is through another; unfortunately it is a public room; therefore, you cannot escape that way without as much risk as you would by going directly out by the door. Don't go that way, but by the window. You see that window?"

Cris looked up.

He had seen the window certainly, and had already looked at it in every possible light, while considering a means of escape, but had come to the conclusion that it wouldn't suit.

In reply he shook his head despairingly.

His visitor seemed to understand him.

"It is too high, perhaps?"

Cris intimated by a sign that the difficulty was not in its height.

"The bars would prevent you getting out?"

The hunter's head nodded like a mandarin's.

"Is that all? Then I may as well tell you—Hush, some one is coming."

One of the sentinels had thrust his head inside the door; he luckily withdrew it, convinced that all was right.

On its disappearance Carrol's mysterious visitor returned and resumed the conversation.

"You think those bars would hinder your escape?"

Another nod was the answer.

"You are mistaken."

The backwoodsman, now perfectly *au fait* with his pantomimic part of the dialogue, gave a modest but expressive look of dissent.

"I tell you you are mistaken," continued the young girl, "they are all sawn through. I see you are curious to know who did that?"

Cris said "yes," without speaking a word.

"It was I!"

"You?" he telegraphed.

"Yes; I was once a close prisoner in this very room, not watched as you are, but still a prisoner. I broke a watch to pieces, took out the mainspring, filed a saw with the nail-cleaning blade of a pen-knife, and with that I sawed away the bars, leaving barely enough to hold them together."

Carrol's look expressed astonishment.

"Yes ; it was hard work, and it took weeks to accomplish it. I daresay you wonder why I didn't make my escape. That's too long a story to tell you now."

The backwoodsman's look was very eloquent, and his visitor equally quick of comprehension.

By that look he asked a question.

"No ; I'm not a prisoner now," she answered, " only in name. You shall have the benefit of my labours. But you must do everything cautiously. And first, to get rid of your guards."

"How is that to be done?"

It was the captive who asked himself this question.

"Here is a bottle," continued she ; " it contains a sleeping draught. When they return, ask them for a drink ; they will give it to you in a gourd ; manage to pour the contents of this bottle into the gourd, and invite them to drink along with you. They will do so, as they never refuse a condemned captive. In a few minutes, the draught will take effect.

"Then climb to the window, remove the bars without noise, let yourself down softly, and make your way straight into the forest. No thanks till I see you again !"

With these words his visitor vanished, the opening in the wall closed noiselessly, and Cris lay wondering whether he had been sleeping or waking, listening to a soft, delicate voice, or only dreaming that he heard it.

The phial in his hand, however, gave token that he had not been dreaming.

His visitor was no creature of another world, but one of this mundane sphere.

The hunter scratched his head with bewilderment, and mentally reviewed the situation.

"Wal, of all the surprisingest things as ever I met, this air the most tremenjous. Bite me to death with gillinippers if ever I thought to have seed sich a thing and not yell right out ! And me a lyin' here when that splendiferous critter war a botherin' her brain to sarve this ole sinner ! It's the most etarnal 'stonishing thing ever heerd on, that's what it is. Yah ! so you're come ag'in, air ye?" he continued, as two of his guards re-entered. "Wal, I reckon I've got somethin' as 'ill suit your complaint. Come in, ye devils, you ! "

The unconscious objects of his apostrophe having entered the room, seated themselves not far from him, chattering with each other. The subject of their conversation was uninteresting to their prisoner, who lay revolving in his mind what was best to be done.

The time for putting his plan into execution had at length arrived.

His sentinels had ceased conversing, and were with difficulty keeping themselves awake.

"Look hyar, redskins," he said, addressing them, " have ye sich a thing as a drop of water? I'm most chokin' with thirst, and I see it's no use waiting till you asks me, so I'll take the trouble off your hands, and ask you."

One of the Indians good-naturedly went outside, returning with a gourd, which he handed to the prisoner.

Cris raised it to his lips, and drank; then paused, as if for breath.

"By the eternal," said he, "if I didn't think I seed one of your comrades put his head in that thar door. What kin he want?"

The men looked in the direction of the door.

The contents of the phial were poured into the gourd.

When the Indians looked again at their captive, he was apparently enjoying another long draught of water.

Not a drop, however, passed his lips.

"Ah!" he exclaimed, after his seemingly exhausting imbibition, and with the greatest difficulty suppressing a grimace, "there's nothing like water to refresh one. It a'most gives a dyin' man new lease o' his life. I wonder I never tried it afore. There's a smack o' freedom about it that's worth its weight in gold. Try it yourselves, and don't stand staring, as if you was a-goin' to swallow me."

The comical expression of their captive's face, more than the long speech he made to the two men, induced them to oblige him.

Putting their lips to the gourd, each took a draught of the water.

They did not seem to coincide with him in his opinion of its virtues.

The old hunter laughed in his sleeve on perceiving their wry faces.

"Don't like it, eh? Wal, you don't know what's good for ye. Poor benighted critters! how should ye?"

As he made the remark, he fell back upon his log bolster, and again seemed to compose himself to sleep.

If the Indians had been somnolent before drinking the water, they were not rendered more wakeful by the indulgence, and it was almost ludicrous to see what useless efforts they made to battle against the potent narcotic.

In vain they talked to each other, got up, and paced the room, and endeavoured to stand up without leaning up against the wall.

This struggle between sleep and watchfulness at length came to a close.

In less than ten minutes after taking the draught, both lay stretched along the floor in a deep, death-like slumber.

The backwoodsman lost no more time.

With an agile motion, he planted his feet in the interstices of the logs, and reached the window.

A slight wrenching of the bars showed the skill with which they had been sawn asunder.

One after another gave way, and the whole framework was in his hands.

He was on the point of dropping it gently, when outside under the window a human form appeared.

It was that of an Indian.

## CHAPTER XXXIX.

### AN OLD ACQUAINTANCE.

N seeing the Indian, Cris Carrol felt himself in a dilemma.

But he did not pause long before taking action.

He saw that the man was not watching him, but seemed to have his eyes fixed upon the windows of the adjoining habitation.

Quietly pulling in the iron framework, which was beginning to feel heavy, Cris deposited it without noise in the interior of the room, and again clambered up to the window. Before doing so, he stole his knife from one of the sleeping sentinels.

The Indian outside had still maintained his attitude.

When Cris looked forth again, he saw him with his eyes fixed on the same spot.

What was to be done?

The only thing that suggested itself to the hunter was precisely what he did do.

He crept through the window.

So quietly, that ere the individual below was aware of his presence, he had seized him by the throat and forced him to the ground.

A surprise awaited him when he had accomplished this feat. The Indian's face was revealed, and, to Carrol's surprise, no less than his joy for not having plunged the knife into his heart, he recognised it.

" Nelatu !"

" Carrol !"

" Hush ! or you'll alarm all the redskins about the place."

" What are you doing here ?"

" I've just dropped out of that window." He pointed to the opening above.

" How came you to go in there ?"

" I didn't go in of my own will, you may bet high on that. I war brung."

" Who brought you ?"

" Some o' y'ur own Injuns."

" A prisoner ?"

" That's about the size of it. I shouldn't have been one much longer."

" What do you mean ?"

" Why, that to-morrow I'd have been as dead as a man could be, with forty or fifty fellows playing blue-blazes on his carcase."

" Ha ! they have decreed on burning you ?"

" That's it, lad, and consarn me if I ain't glad to be out hyar in the open air a-tellin' it you, 'stead of in there a-thinkin' of it."

"Who condemned you?"

"Wal, names hev a kind o' slipped my memory, but they wur warriors and braves of y'ur enlightened community."

"Why did you not send for me?"

"I thought of that, but they told me you war gone, and wouldn't be back in time for the ceremony."

"How did you get out here? Who opened the window?"

"That war done by a angel."

"An angel?—what do you mean?"

"Jist this; that at one of the corners of that thar eternal hole, a angel appeared and showed me the road to liberty."

"Who was it?"

"Wal, it air no use keepin' it from you——"

"Speak! who was it?"

"I'll tell you, but first listen a spell to somethin' else. Nelatu, lad, I once did you a sarvice."

"You did! I shall never forget it!"

"Durn it, it warn't for that I made mention on't. It war only this—look me in the face, and tell me on the word of a man, you mean square with me. Do that, an' I'll put my trust in ye, as I'm now puttin' my life in your hands."

"Upon an Indian warrior's word, I am your friend!"

"You air, Nelatu? Then dog-gorn me if I doubt you. Your hand!"

They exchanged a friendly grasp.

"It is more nor my life—it am the name and actions of the most ⋯iferous, angeliferous critter the ⋯ set eyes on! It air——"

Rody!"

⋯ showed some surprise as the name.

"Yes, it war that same gal; but how on airth did you come for to guess it so straight?"

"Because that one name is never absent from my thoughts."

The hunter uttered a strange exclamation.

"Ho-ho!" he muttered to himself, "the wind sits in that quarter, do it? Poor lad, I'm fear'd thar ain't no chance for him."

"I fear it," said Nelatu, overhearing the muttered remark; "but, come!—what she has commenced I will accomplish. At all risks I shall assist you in regaining your liberty."

"Wal, I'll be glad to get it."

"Then follow me!"

The Indian rapidly crossed the open space at the back of the house, and led the way to the edge of the forest.

The released captive strode silently after.

They paused under a grove of live-oaks, in the shadow of which Carrol perceived a horse.

"It is yours," said Nelatu; "follow the straight path and you are free."

"Nelatu," said the backwoodsman, "you've done me a great service. I'm goin' to give you a bit of advice in return for it.

"Give up the angeliferous crittur that's your prisoner; send her back to her own people, and forget her!"

"If I could forget her, you mean."

"Wal, I don't know much myself about them thar things; only my advice is—Give her up! You'll be a deal happier," he added, suddenly waxing impassioned. "That 'ere gal am as much above either you or me, or the likes of us, as the genooine angels air above all mortals. Therefore give her up, lad—give her up!"

Again pressing Nelatu's hand in his, the old hunter climbed into the saddle, gave a kick to the horse, and rode off a free man.

"Kim up, ye Seminole critter!" said he to the animal he bestrode, "an' take me once more to the open savannas; for, durn me! if this world arn't gettin' mixed up so that it's hard for a poor ignorant fellar like me to know whether them that call 'emselves civilized air more to be thought on than them that air savages, or *wisey wersey*."

The question was one that has puzzled clearer brains than those of Cris Carrol.

## CHAPTER XL.

### THE TALE OF AN INDIAN CHIEF.

S the old hunter has ridden out of our sight and for ever, let us return to the Indian town where Alice Rody was so strangely domiciled.

Her people had buried the ill-fated Sansuta near the old fort.

The wild flowers she had loved so well had already blossomed over her grave.

Wacora and Nelatu had both been present—both much afflicted.

The events of the contest had called them away immediately afterwards. Wacora remained absent, but his cousin had made a stolen visit to the town, as shown by the incidents already related.

The search for the escaped captive was carried on for some time with vigour, but was at length abandoned.

Meanwhile the other captive's life passed without incident. The aid she had given the backwoodsman had afforded her the greatest pleasure.

She had been informed of his capture immediately after his condemnation, and was resolved to help him in his escape.

She did not know of Nelatu's presence near the scene, nor of his well-timed assistance.

The Indian youth had ridden many miles that evening, merely to stand and gaze at her window.

To feel that he was near her seemed a happiness to him.

He departed without even seeing her.

Weeks had elapsed since the Indian maiden had been laid to rest within the old fort.

Alice often visited the spot.

And there Wacora, who had once more returned to the town again, saw her.

She was resting on the same stone where Sansuta's head had rested on her bosom.

On perceiving the chief's approach, she rose to her feet as if to quit the spot.

"Does my coming drive you away?" he asked.

"Not that; but it is growing late, and I must return to my prison."

"Your prison?"

"Is it not my prison?"

"It is no more your prison than you are a prisoner. You have long been free."

There was a mournful sadness in Alice Rody's speech which touched the heart of the Indian chief.

"Freedom is a boon only to those who can enjoy it," she said, after a pause.

"And you are unhappy?" asked Wacora.

"Can you ask that question?—you who have done so much——" She paused; her generous nature hesitated to inflict pain.

He concluded her speech for her.

"I who have done so much to make you unhappy. You are right. I have been an instrument in the hands of Fate, and you owe your misery to me. But I am only an instrument, not the original cause. My will had no voice in my actions, and but one motive prompted me. That was Duty!"

"Duty?" she asked, a smile curling her lip.

"Yes, Duty! I could prove it to you had you the desire to hear me."

She resumed her seat, and said quietly—

"I will hear you."

"There was an Indian chief, the son of a Spanish woman. His father was a Seminole. Both are dead. He was reared amongst his father's people, and learned from them all that Indian youths are taught. Schools then existed amongst the Seminoles. The white missionaries had established them, and were still at their heads. They had both the ability and the desire to teach. From them Wacora learned all that the pale-faced children are taught. His mind was of his mother's race; his heart inclined to that of his father's.

"But why this difference?" she asked.

"Because the more he knew the more was he convinced of the cruel oppression that had been suffered in all ages. History was a tissue of it. Geography marked its progress. Education only proved that civilisation was spread at the expense of honour and of right. This is what the schools taught him."

"That is one side of the question."

"You are right; so he resolved to make himself familiar with the other. The story of the past might be inapplicable to the events of the present. Believing this he left the schools, and sought the savanna and the forest. What did he find there? Nothing but the repetition of that past he had read of in books, aggravated by the lawlessness and rapacity of the present. The red-man was ignorant. But did the pale-faces seek to educate him? No! They sought and still seek to keep him ignorant, because, in his ignorance, lies their advantage."

"Was that all the fault of our race?" Alice asked, as she noticed the enthusiastic flush upon the speaker's face.

"Not all. That were to argue falsely. The red man's vices grew greater as the chances of correcting them were denied him. His instinct prompted him to retaliation, for by this he sought to check oppression. 'Twas a vain effort. He found it so; and was forced to practise cruelty. So the quarrel progressed, till to-day the Indian warrior sees in every white man only an enemy."

"But now? Surely you are not so?"

"I am the Indian chief I have attempted to describe. Take that for your answer."

The young girl was silent.

"If my heart bleeds for suffering, it is my mother's nature pleading within me. I check it, because it would be unworthy of a warrior, and the leader of warriors. The storm has arisen—I am carried along with it!"

As he uttered the last words his form seemed to dilate, while his listener stood wondering at it spell bound.

After a pause he continued, in a tone more subdued, but still full of feeling—

"If I have caused you unhappiness, think of me as the involuntary instrument. My uncle was beloved by all his tribe—by all our race. His injuries were ours, it was ours to avenge them. And for her"—his voice trembled, as he pointed to Sansuta's grave—"*she* was his only hope and joy upon earth."

Alice Rody's tears fell in torrents over the last resting-place of the Indian maiden. Wacora observed them, and, with a delicacy of feeling, was about to withdraw from her presence, when she stayed him with a motion of her hand.

For some time neither uttered a word. Alice at length spoke, through sobs which she vainly strove to check or conceal,

"Forgive me!" said she, "for I have done you a great wrong. Much that was dark and terrible appears now just and natural. I cannot say that I am happier, but I am less troubled than before."

He would have kissed her hand, but with a slight shudder she drew back.

"No, no; do not touch me! Leave me to myself. I shall be more composed by-and-bye."

He obeyed, without saying a word; leaving her alone.

For a long time she sat in the same place, a prey to thoughts she scarce understood.

At length she rose, to all appearance more composed, and retracing the forest path with slow, sad steps, she re-entered the Indian town.

## CHAPTER XLI.

### A TREACHEROUS BRIDGE.

HERE was one among the Indians who viewed their fair captive with no great favour.

It was Maracota.

His devotion to Oluski had been so blindly true that, in his narrow-minded memory of the old chief's wrongs, he had become bloodthirsty and remorseless. Naturally of a revengeful disposition, he saw, in the leniency of both Wacora and Nelatu towards the pale-faced maiden, too much of forgiveness.

This stirred his evil passions to their depth, and he sought for an opportunity to do her an injury.

With a shrewd guess at the truth, he looked upon Cris Carrol's escape as another evidence of that toleration which ill consorted with his sanguinary hatred of the white race.

He dared not take open measures, but insidiously strove to turn the people of the tribe against their white captive as well as Wacora.

His success was not commensurate with his wishes. They admired their chief too much to believe anything to his prejudice, and Maracota became himself looked upon as a restless agitator—a subject more zealous than loyal.

He saw, accordingly, that any injury to the captive must be accomplished by his own agency; the more so, as he had already endeavoured to excite a feeling of jealousy in Nelatu's mind of which she and Wacora were the objects. The generous youth not only refused belief, but angrily reproved the slanderer, for daring to couple his cousin's name with an act so unworthy !

When a person resolves upon mischief it is astonishing how many opportunities present themselves.

Alice, although unsuspicious of the enmity of which she was the object, avoided Maracota. She did so from a different motive. She knew that it was he who had fired the fatal shot at her brother; and could not help regarding the act with abhorrence. His sister, how could she ?

And as his sister, how could she look upon his executioner without repugnance—without horror ?

The exigencies of the war had kept Maracota away from the town, and for long periods ; but the same causes that brought Wacora back, also controlled his return.

He felt that now, if ever, was the time to carry out his schemes of malignity.

He accordingly watched her every movement; amongst others, the many lonely visits she paid to the ruined fort.

There was the opportunity he wanted, if he could only find the means to avail himself of it.

In a community of red-men, where everything is reduced, even in times of a temporary peace, to dull routine, it was not difficult to devise a plan of revenge. But it must be unnoticed, or go unpunished, for he had a wholsome dread of Wacora's displeasure, and was not disposed to incur it.

Some days had elapsed since the intended interview between the chief and his captive, during which time they had seen nothing more of each other.

Wacora, with great delicacy, had avoided her, and she had kept herself within the dwelling assigned to her, afraid to meet him, yet pondering deeply over what he had said.

In spite of a natural prejudice against the Indian race, she was startled and wonder-stricken at the nobility of thought and rare talent he had exhibited.

She did not doubt but that a portion, at least, of his argument was based on false reasoning, but she was not subtle enough, or perhaps indisposed, to detect the erroneous argument. We are very apt to acknowledge the truth of what we admire, whilst admitting its errors.

Alice Rody was in this predicament.

She had learned to respect the Indian chief, and her respect was tinged with admiration of his many good qualities.

This mental ratiocination had occupied her during the days of her seclusion.

She endeavoured to divert her mind to other subjects, and to this end deter-mined to pay another visit to the old fort. She was prompted to it by a thought of having too long forgotten the Indian maiden who slept within the ruins.

It was a glorious morning as she set forth for a walk to the place.

The way was through a belt of timbered land leading to a creek, spanned by a rude wooden bridge. On the other side lay the ruin.

The wood was passed in safety, and she reached the water's edge. To her amazement she found the creek greatly swollen; this often happened after heavy rains, though she had never before seen it in that condition.

She proceeded along the causeway leading to the bridge, that seemed to offer a safe means of crossing.

She paused to contemplate the current, bearing upon its bosom the torn trunks of trees caught in its rapid course.

In another moment she was upon the bridge, and had got midway over it, when a tremulous motion of the planks caused her to hesitate. As she stood still the motion ceased, and smiling at her fears, she again proceeded.

Not far, however. Ere she had made three steps forward, to her horror the motion recommenced with greater violence.

She saw it was too late to retreat, and sped onward, the planks swaying fearfully towards the water.

Believing it best to proceed, she took courage for a fresh effort, and kept on towards the other side. It was a fatal resolution.

Just as the had prepared for her last spring, the planks gave way with a creaking sound, and she was precipitated into the stream.

Her presence of mind was gone, and in an instant she was submerged beneath the seething current of the flood.

She rose again, gave utterance to a shriek, and was again swallowed up, her wail of agony being uttered in the water.

At that moment a face that expressed fiendish delight appeared through the bushes on the bank; nor did it vanish until assured that all was over, and Alice Rody was below the surface, never more to return to it alive.

Then, and not till then, the form emerged from out the underwood, and scrambling to the rude pier from which the planks had parted, stood surveying the scene.

It was Maracota!

"Good!" cried he. "So perish all who would make the red-man forgive the injuries of his race. She was the child of a villain—the sister of a fiend!"

He stooped down and examined the broken fragments of the bridge.

"Maracota's axe has done the deed well," said he, continuing his soliloquy, "and he has nothing to fear. Her death will be attributed to accident. It was a great thought, and one that Oluski's spirit will approve. Maracota was his favourite warrior, and to please his shade has he done this deed, and will do more. Death to the pale-faces —death to their women and children! Death and extermination to the accursed race!"

The vengeful warrior rose from his stooping position, cast one hurried glance upon the turbulent stream, and once more entering the underwood, disappeared from the spot.

# CHAPTER XLII.

### SAVED !

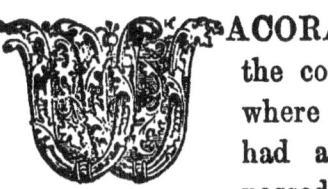WACORA came from the council chamber, where the warriors had assembled, and passed over to the house where dwelt his white captive.

This was no unusual thing for him when he deemed himself safe from her observation. Upon the day in question, however, he had resolved to see her.

The time had come when active measures were about to be taken by the United States Government in order to " suppress " (such was the term used) the Indians in Florida, and although none could know at that moment how difficult the undertaking would prove, all were alive to the fact that the work was about to commence in earnest.

Information of this had reached the young Seminole chief; and he saw the necessity of removing his tribe from their present residence.

Hence the council—hence, also, his visit to Alice Rody.

He had determined to lay the facts fully before her, in order that she might name the time of return to her own people.

Thus reflecting, he walked on towards the house tenanted by his captive.

On arriving at the place he found she was not there; but some children playing near told him she had gone into the woods, and pointed in the direction she had taken.

The young chief hesitated about following her.

He was unwilling to thrust himself into her presence at a time she had, perhaps, devoted to self communion and repose.

Turning in another direction, he wandered for some time purposelessly, taking no note of the locality, until he had reached the belt of woods which Alice had herself traversed on her road to the old ruin. Wacora, however, entered it at some distance farther off from the skirts of the town.

Once under the shadows of the trees he abated his pace, which, up to this time, had been rapid.

Now walking with slow step, and abstracted air, he finally stopped and leant against a huge live-oak, his eyes wandering afar over the sylvan scene.

" Here," he soliloquised in thought, " here, away from men and their doings, alone is there peace ! How my heart sickens at the thought that human ambitions and human vanities should so pervert man's highest mission—peace —turning the world into scenes of strife and bloodshed! I, an Indian savage, as white men call me, would gladly lay down this day and for ever the rifle and the knife; would willingly bury the war hatchet, and abandon this sanguinary contest!

"Could I do so with honour?" he asked, after a pause of reflection. "No! To the end I must now proceed. I see the end with a prophetic eye; but I must go on as I've begun, even if my tribe with all our people should be swept from the earth! Fool that I've been to covet the leadership of a forlorn hope!"

At the end of this soliloquy he stamped the ground with fury.

Petty dissensions had arisen among the people he deemed worthy of the highest form of liberty.

By this his temper had been chafed —his hopes suddenly discouraged. He was but partaking of the enthusiast's fate, finding the real so unlike the ideal. It is the penalty usually paid by intelligence when it seeks to reform or better the condition of fallen humanity.

"And she," he continued, in his heart's bitterness, "she can only think of me as a vain savage; vain of the slight superiority education appears to give me over others of my race. I might as well aspire to make my home among the stars as in her bosom. She is just as distant, or as unlikely to be mine."

In the mood in which the Indian was at that moment, the whole universe seemed leagued against him.

Bitterly he lamented the fate that had given him grand inspirations, while denying him their enjoyment.

As he stood beneath the spreading branches of the live-oak, a double shadow seemed to have fallen upon him—that of his own thoughts, and the tree thickly festooned with its mosses. Both were of sombre hue.

He took no heed of the time, and might have stood nursing his bitter thoughts still longer, but for a sound that suddenly startled him from his reverie.

It was a shriek that came ringing through the trees as if of one in great distress.

The voice Wacora heard was a woman's. Loverlike, he knew it to be that of Alice Rody in peril.

Without hesitating an instant, he rushed along the path in the direction from which it appeared to come.

In that direction lay the stream.

His instinct warned him that the danger was from the water. He remembered the rain and storm just past. It would be followed by a freshet. Alice Rody might have been caught by it, and was in danger of drowning.

He made these reflections while rushing through the underwood, careless of the thorns that at every step penetrated his skin, covering his garments with blood.

His demeanour had become suddenly changed. The sombre shadow on his brow had given place to an air of the wildest excitement. His white captive, she who had made him a captive, was in some strange peril.

He listened as he ran. The swishing

of the branches, as he broke through them, hindered him from hearing. No sound reached his ears; but he saw what caused him a strange surprise. It was the form of a man, who, like himself, was making his way through the thicket, only in a different direction. Instead of towards the creek, the man was going from it, skulking off as if desirous to shun observation.

For all this Wacora recognised him. He saw it was Maracota.

The young chief did not stay to inquire what the warrior was doing there, or why he should be retreating from the stream. He did not even summon the latter to stop. His thoughts were all absorbed by the shriek he had heard, and the danger it denoted. He felt certain it had come from the creek, and if it was the cry of one in the water, there was no time to be lost.

And none was lost—not a moment—for in less than sixty seconds after hearing it he stood upon the bank of the stream.

As he had anticipated, it was swollen to a flood, its turbid waters carrying upon their whirling surface trunks and torn branches of trees, bunches of reeds, and grass uprooted by the rush of the current.

He did not stand to gaze idly upon these. The bridge was above him. The cry had come from there. He saw that it was in ruins. All was explained!

But where was she who had given utterance to that fearful shriek?

He hurried along the edge of the stream, scanning its current from bank to bank, hastily examining every branch and bunch borne upon its bosom.

A disc of whitish colour came before his eyes. There was something in the water, carried along rapidly. It was the drapery of a woman's dress, and a woman's form was within it!

The young chief stayed not for further scrutiny; but, plunging into the flood, and swimming a few strokes, he threw his arms around it.

And he knew that in those arms he held Alice Rody. In a few seconds after her form lay dripping upon the bank, apparently lifeless.

## CHAPTER XLIII.

### DEATH OF NELATU.

HE Indian chief had saved his white captive. She still lived!

The struggle between life and death had been long and doubtful, but life at length triumphed.

For days she lingered upon the verge of existence, powerless to move from her couch—scarce able to speak. It was some time before she could shape words to thank her deliverer, though she knew who it was.

She had been told it was Wacora.

The young chief was unremitting in his attentions, and showed great solicitude for her recovery. He found time, amidst the warlike preparations constantly going on, to make frequent calls at her dwelling, and make anxious inquiry about her progress.

The nurses who attended upon her did not fail to notice his anxiety.

Nelatu had been absent, and did not return to the town until she was convalescent.

He was grieved to the heart on hearing what had happened.

Wacora, suspecting that Maracota was the guilty one, sought him in every direction, but the vengeful warrior was nowhere to be found.

He had fled from the presence of his indignant chief.

It was not until long after that his fate became known.

He had been captured in his flight by some of the settlers, and shot; thus dying by the hands of enemies he so hated.

Several weeks elapsed, and no active movement had, as yet, been made by the government troops. Wacora's tribe had still continued to reside in their town undisturbed.

His captive continued to recover, and along with her restored strength, came a change over the spirit of her existence. She seemed transformed into a different being.

The past had vanished like a dream. Only dimly did she remember her residence at Tampa Bay—her father, the conflict on the hill, the massacre, her brother's sad fate—all seemed to have faded from her memory, until they appeared as things that had never been, or of which she had no personal knowledge, but had only heard of them long, long ago.

It is true they still had a shadowy existence in her mind, but entirely disassociated with the events of her life, since she had been a captive among the

Indians. Nor was there much to regret in this impaired recollection, for both the events and personages had been among the miseries of her life.

Of her present she had a more pleasurable appreciation. She was living a new life, and thinking new thoughts.

Nelatu and Wacora both strove in a thousand kind ways to render her contented and happy.

They had no great luxuries to offer her, but such as they had were bestowed with true delicacy.

Strange to say, that in this common solicitude there was not a spark of jealousy between the two cousins.

Nelatu's nature was generosity itself; and self-sacrifice appeared to him as if it was his duty or fate.

Still, while he basked in the sunshine of the young girl's beauty, he had not the courage to imagine to himself that she could ever belong to another. Not to him might her love be given, but surely not to another! He could not think of that.

True that at times he fancied he could perceive a look bestowed on Wacora such as she never vouchsafed to him—a tremor in her voice when speaking to his cousin, which had never betrayed itself in her discourse with himself.

But he might be mistaken.

Might?

He was certain of it.

If she did not love him, at any rate he could not think that she loved Wacora.

Thus did the Indian youth beguile himself!

Innocent as a child, he knew little of the heart of woman.

That look—that tremor of the voice should have told him that she loved Wacora.

Yes; the end had come, and love had conquered.

The white maiden was in love with the young Indian chief!

\*    \*    \*    \*    \*

Wacora and his captive—now more than ever his captive—were seated within the ruined fort near Sansuta's grave.

"You are pleased once more to be here?" he asked.

"I am. During my illness I promised myself, if ever I recovered, that my first visit should be to this spot."

"And yet it was in paying such a visit that you nearly lost your life."

"The life you saved."

"'Twas a happy chance. I cannot tell what led me to the forest on that occasion."

"What were you doing there?" she asked.

"Like the blind mortal that I am, I was blaming myself, and my fate, too, when I should have been blessing my fortune."

"For what?"

"For conducting me to the spot where I heard your cry."

"What fortune were you blaming?"

"That which made me unworthy."

"Unworthy of what?"

He did not immediately answer her, but the look he gave her caused her to turn her eyes to the ground.

"Do you really wish to know of what I think myself unworthy?"

She smiled as she replied—

"If you betray no confidence in telling me."

"None ; none but my own."

"Then tell me if you like."

Was it the faint tremor in her voice that emboldened him to speak ?

"Unworthy of *you !*" was his answer.

"Of me ?" she said, her face averted from his.

"Of you, and you only. But why should I withhold further confidence ? You have given me courage to speak ; have I also your leave ?"

She made no answer to the last question, but her look was eloquent of assent.

"I thought on that day," he continued, "that I was accursed by man and Heaven ; that I, an Indian savage, was not accounted worthy to indulge in thoughts of love that had sprung up within my heart, like a pure flower, only to be blighted by the prejudices of race; that all my adoration for the fair and excellent must be kept down by the accident of birth ; and that, whilst nurturing a holy passion, I must crush it out and stifle it for ever."

"But now !" Her voice was low and tremulous.

"Now all rests upon one word.

Upon one word depends my happiness or misery now and for ever."

"And what is it ?"

"Do not ask it from me. It must come from your eyes—from your lips—from your heart !"

There was an eloquence that spoke the answer without a word being uttered.

It was the eloquence of love !

In another instant the lips of the white maiden touched those of her Indian lover.

From their rapturous embrace they were startled by a sound.

It was a groan !

It came from the other side of Sansuta's grave, behind which there was a clump of bushes.

Wacora rushed towards the spot, while Alice kept her place transfixed to it by a terrible presentiment.

The young chief uttered an exclamation of horror, as he looked in among the bushes.

His cousin was lying beneath them, stretched out—dead ; a dagger, which his right hand still clutched, sheathed in his heart.

With his last groan, and his heart's blood, the generous youth had yielded up his love with his life.